CW00433729

PRAISE FOR
The Vanishing Act

SHORTLISTED FOR THE 2012 COMMONWE⎯ ⎯⎯⎯ ⊔ĸ ᴘʀɪᴢᴇ

'A perfectly poised, fable-like tale of loss, written with
delightful whimsy, deep empathy and a beguiling sense
of innocence. This book is a gem.' Graeme Base

'A beautiful, moving fable. *The Vanishing Act* is one of the
best books I have read in a long time.' Eva Hornung

'This book is a precious thing. I want to keep it in a painted
box with a raven feather and sea-polished stones, taking it out
when I feel the need to visit Minou on her island again. The best
stories change you. I am not the same after *The Vanishing Act*.'
Erin Morgenstern, author of *The Night Circus*

'Mette Jakobsen's first novel is a gossamer web, a work
of fragile beauty...a delightfully rendered portrayal of
innocence coping with loss, of someone who has found
a great deal to explore in a tiny space.' *Age*

'Jakobsen's European sensibility is apparent...[her] prose is
stylish and she works with some fine imagery.' *Australian*

'This book is a sharp, elegantly written fable about loss,
loneliness and taking comfort in what you have. The characters
are redolent of some of Hemingway or Steinbeck's best. *The
Vanishing Act*, surely one of the more adventurous Australian
novels of the year, is a pleasure.' *Sunday Mail Brisbane*

'A stunning new voice for fans of literary fiction.'
Books+Publishing

'Jakobsen's debut novel is a delectable delight, a fetching
fable that is both heartbreaking in its poignancy and
breathtaking in its delicacy.' *Booklist*

Mette Jakobsen was born in Copenhagen, Denmark, and now lives in Newtown, Sydney. She has a PhD in Creative Writing and a BA in philosophy. In 2004 she graduated from NIDA's Playwrights Studio and several of her plays have been broadcast on ABC Radio National. Her novels are *The Vanishing Act*, shortlisted for the Commonwealth Book Prize in 2012, and *What the Light Hides*.

What the Light Hides

METTE JAKOBSEN

TEXT PUBLISHING MELBOURNE AUSTRALIA

textpublishing.com.au

The Text Publishing Company
Swann House
22 William Street
Melbourne Victoria 3000
Australia

© Mette Jakobsen 2016

The moral right of Mette Jakobsen to be identified as the author of this work has been asserted.

All rights reserved. Without limiting the rights under copyright above, no part of this publication shall be reproduced, stored in or introduced into a retrieval system, or transmitted in any form or by any means (electronic, mechanical, photocopying, recording or otherwise) without the prior permission of both the copyright owner and publisher of this book.

First published in Australia by The Text Publishing Company, 2016

Book and cover design by Imogen Stubbs
Cover photograph by Whitney Ott / Offset
Typesetting by J&M Typesetting

Printed in Australia by Griffin Press, an Accredited ISO AS/NZS 14001:2004 Environmental Management System Printer

National Library of Australia Cataloguing-in-Publication entry

Creator: Jakobsen, Mette, 1964–.
Title: What the light hides / by Mette Jakobsen.
ISBN: 9781922079299 (paperback)
ISBN: 9781921921438 (ebook)
Subjects: Parental grief—Fiction.
             Bereavement—Fiction.
             Man–woman relationships—Fiction.
Dewey Number: A823.4

This book is printed on paper certified against the Forest Stewardship Council® Standards. Griffin Press holds FSC chain-of-custody certification SGS-COC-005088. FSC promotes environmentally responsible, socially beneficial and economically viable management of the world's forests.

For Kirsten

Night still floats in the morning light. A thick and watery presence of shades and depth, of dreams and slow heart-beats. Outside our bedroom window I can see the hazy shapes of the hedges, the wild rosebushes, the long grass and the oak. I am guessing there is frost on the grass. It's winter in Mount Wilson.

Vera is asleep next to me, her arm flung above her head, her breath deep and steady. For a moment I pretend that nothing has changed, that when she wakes she will look at me the way she did before. I pull on a jumper and walk down the chilly corridor to the kitchen. I don't turn on the light before filling the kettle. I don't mind the grey darkness; I know the house inside out. We have lived here for more than twenty years. Vera and I. And Ben.

I sit at the kitchen table and look out onto the garden while I wait for the water to boil.

I loved her name straight away. Vera. It's old-fashioned, but it suits her. The first time I saw her was at a dinner party hosted in a warehouse in the inner city. I noticed her instantly. She had long hair then too and she was beautiful, but it was her dress that caught my eye. It was turquoise and shimmering, cut deep in front, and it seemed a bit too big for her. It looked like something pulled out of the dress-up box; a bit too loud and a bit too vintage for the black-clad crowd. But it wasn't just the dress that made me watch her throughout dinner. It was the way she observed her surroundings: the people, the food, the bare grey walls. She observed it all openly, curiously, as if she wasn't quite part of the scene. Halfway through the first course Vera caught my eye across the table. She lifted her glass in a toast and drank without breaking eye contact.

The person next to me told me that the warehouse had been an old flour mill and he had looked admiringly at the bare walls through black-rimmed glasses. I found the space pretentious and cold. If it hadn't been for the lamps—floating orbs of opaque glass—it would have been an entirely miserable place. There were fifteen of them hanging at different heights and the light was so exquisite that for a moment I considered abandoning my work with wood for glass.

I am rarely shy, but that night after dinner I felt an overwhelming shyness seeing Vera walk towards me. Chet

Baker was playing 'Almost Blue' on the stereo. The lamps were dimmed and the tables moved up against the wall to make space for what the host called 'intimate little gatherings'. Waiters were weaving between guests with champagne and I was standing by myself at the coffee table.

'You like to be alone,' she said as she reached me. Her voice was warm.

A waiter stopped to offer her a glass of champagne and she regarded it with the same inquiring look she had everything else that evening. Her hair fell to her waist, her dress sparkled and I thought she was extraordinarily beautiful.

I toasted her glass lightly with my coffee cup. 'And you like to watch,' I said, realising it sounded wrong, but not knowing how else to put it.

They could have been lines out of a surrealist play. They would have sat comfortably in the dialogue of *Waiting for Godot*, which I saw once without understanding a word of it.

We kept talking, but I don't remember what we said. It was stray lines, fragments that didn't mean anything. All I remember is that I couldn't take my eyes off her and when she put her hand in mine in a way that was neither casual nor intentionally seductive I embarrassed myself by getting an erection so violent that it threatened to make me pass out.

We went back to my place and barely made it through

the door. I broke the rusted zipper on her dress in the hall-way and found out in the process that the soft material smelled of mothballs. We ended up on the floor next to my work boots and a spare bike wheel. I came almost immedi-ately and she moments after, guiding my hand. I had never experienced anyone receiving me with such abandon and complete confidence. Afterwards my body felt raw, but not spent. I was hungry for her in a way I hadn't felt before and every time I had her after that the hunger grew. I tasted those long fingers, the curve of her waist, the inside of her, and it was never enough.

The kettle boils and I can hear Vera in the shower, but I don't get up just yet. It's almost light outside. As I predicted there is frost on the grass. It will disappear when the sun comes out, but the cold will remain throughout the day.

Ours is one of the oldest houses in Mount Wilson. It dates back to the beginning of the twentieth century, when early settlers escaped the hot Sydney summers in favour of a cool temperate climate. The European trees planted then stand tall in the rich volcanic soil among lilli pilli, sassa-fras, coachwood and ferns.

People come up from the city for the weekend. They cruise past beautiful gardens and sandstone fences. Sometimes they get out of the car on wobbly city legs and stretch as if they have endured days of driving. Our garden falls short. It sits behind a peeling wooden fence with flowers that neither Vera nor I know the names of and grass that is permanently too long. Even Vera's rose garden is so wild that it could be the setting of a fairytale. The stalks crawl up fences and wind along the ground with thorns thick and sharp. Our neighbour Rob says every chance he gets: 'Every town needs an artist.' But by the tone of his voice it's clear he believes that our street suffers because of it.

Something moves at the back of the garden. I lean closer to the window. It's a lyrebird. For a moment its curly tail feathers stand in relief against the wall of Vera's studio. Then it's gone, back into the bush.

I get up when I hear Vera leave the bathroom. I make coffee while listening to the news on the radio, I do all the same things I did five months ago.

Before it happened.

It was summer then and just like today I got up first. Vera appeared after her shower with bare feet and wet hair, wearing her faded blue kimono. She popped bread in the toaster, carried cheese and butter to the table, and I brushed her waist as we passed each other in our familiar routine. We had spent that early morning making love and I felt hot and weak in the knees and thought to myself, *You lucky, lucky bugger.* She caught me looking at her and laughed in that soft way of hers. I laughed too and considered taking her right back to bed.

'No,' she said as I reached for her, 'don't even think about it, darling. I'm going to the studio.' She looked out the window and spotted Earl, the postman, at the end of the driveway. 'Pour me a coffee instead.'

I saw her sidestepping the sharp stones on our driveway and Earl handing her a bunch of letters. I poured coffee thinking about the work I needed to complete that day. I was working on what I called my ghost table. It was made from the lightest shade of grey maple. The customer lived in an architecturally designed glass house right on Pebble Beach on the south coast and I knew the table would fit the white driftwood and the grey pebbles perfectly.

When Vera came back inside she looked different.

'What?' I put my cup down. 'What's the matter?'

'There's a letter for Ben.'

It happened from time to time that letters arrived for him at our address, even though he'd lived and studied in the city for almost four years.

'What's the letter?' I asked.

'A dental reminder.'

'So?' I said.

She stared at the envelope, then back up at me. 'I haven't been able to get hold of him all week.'

I handed her a cup of coffee, reminding myself to bring

an extra set of sheets to the workshop. The timber had bruised slightly the day before and I had to take extra care. 'It's the first week back at uni, he's probably busy,' I said.

'David,' she reached for her phone, 'I have the strangest feeling.'

'He was fine at your exhibition,' I said. I felt a sting from the memory. 'He was so fine, in fact, he managed to ignore me all night.'

Vera touched my cheek and managed a half-smile as she dialled his number. The sun caught her bare feet and the edge of the kimono. I heard the muted sound of Ben's voice on the answering machine and then the beep.

'Ben, darling,' Vera said. 'I'm worried about you. Please call as soon as you get this, call me this morning.' She hung up and looked at me. 'He's all right, isn't he?' she asked.

'Of course he is,' I said.

It's five months since that morning and everything has changed. Time doesn't heal. Sometimes I feel so awful I just want to die and on other days I am filled with a wild, furious hope that things are not what they seem, that somehow the coroner made a mistake.

This morning Vera appears in the kitchen ready for work in boots, jeans and a jumper. Her hair is in a ponytail and a scarf is wrapped around her neck.

She walks over to the window. 'Frost,' she says.

I want to tell her that I am thinking of going away for a while, but instead I say, 'There was a lyrebird in the garden before.'

She doesn't ask where I had seen it or what it looked like.

Our days are filled with silence; we barely talk and when we do we mostly argue. We haven't made love for a long time. Not since before the funeral.

Later I watch Vera walk across the lawn. Light appears in her studio, soft in the grey morning. I don't know what she does all day. She hasn't worked on anything since Ben disappeared.

I stay in the kitchen a little longer and by the time I walk around the house to the converted garage the frost has disappeared. I rub Ginger the cat's scruffy head and make sure that she has food and water. Then I put ruler and pencil in my back pocket and get to work.

The smell of timber and glue mingles with the insistent eucalyptus scent from the bush. The garage is freezing and my breath hangs in the air, but I won't feel the cold once I start working.

I have done my best work here. If I dreamed of anything before meeting Vera it was a house like ours: the rustic charm, the light, the sheer freedom of having work and living space all in one. Whenever I've been away and drive back through Bells Line, the last stretch of barren mountain before reaching the village, I feel that I am coming home in the truest sense of the word.

The work set out for me this morning is simple. I am finishing off a four-seater table in mulberry. The tabletop needs paring down and its corners more shape before I apply oil. I start working the medium plane while feeling the wood with my other hand. The work is always tactile. I can trust my hands, but I can't always trust my sight.

The order came through my agent, who is constantly pleading with me to hire an assistant. But I don't want to delegate. Each step in making a piece of furniture is important and part of a whole, even the dull bits, even the sanding.

I've never regretted dropping out of uni to do woodwork. On my worst days in the workshop I am more content than I ever was in lecture halls and with my head buried in books.

I took to it quickly. The tools and the steps involved made sense to me. I went to Japan and spent three months sitting on the floor of a carpentry workshop in Tokyo, where I learned the intricate process of joinery. I almost did my knees in, but it was worth it. By the time I returned to Australia I'd let go of using glue and nails and had a strong vision for my future work. Later I fell in love with inlays.

Not the traditional ones—neat arrangements of flowers and leaves—but bold designs of squares and triangles.

I shift planes, go one smaller and try not to think of Ben. I slow down, continually feeling the wood as I go along. Carpentry is not a wrestle with substance, at least not the way Vera works with metal. Wood can't be conquered; it requires patience and persistence.

I try to let the work guide my thoughts, but it's getting increasingly difficult these days. I am reminded of Ben everywhere I look. This morning the bleak sun falls through the open garage door and I remember him, sitting on the floor in a ray of sun: three years old, playing with wooden blocks. And memory skips in painful staccato. The two of us on a blanket sharing lunch, teaspoons and glasses glinting in the light. Then him, napping on the old lounge in the corner. It was an ordinary morning. A perfectly ordinary morning.

In my memory he is as present as he has always been, and it makes no sense to me that he is dead.

'You have to accept that he is gone,' Vera said last time we argued.

'I do. I do accept it,' I replied.

But Vera knows. She knows that deep down I'm still waiting for him to walk back into our lives with the same carefree attitude he has always had.

The wood shifts under my hands and I stop planing

and reach for the sandpaper.

I stay in the workshop all day. Late afternoon I walk back to the house. The feeble winter sun never makes it past the thick walls and the house is cold and dark. I turn the lights on in the kitchen and make a sandwich with cheese and lettuce. I add extra butter, even though I should probably watch my weight, and I eat standing in the living room at a loss for what to do next. The evenings are the worst. Some nights we go to bed early just to avoid the silence, but more often than not we end up lying awake next to each other, listening to the croaky hoots of the frogmouth owl that lives in Rob's tall pines.

I take another bite of my sandwich and look around the room. A beautiful but worn Persian rug covers the floor. A comfortable lounge sits next to the fireplace and above the lounge hangs the painting that we bought in Moscow on our honeymoon. We both love it. It's dramatic and dreamy at the same time, depicting a tower in mid-fall. Parts float in a pale blue sky: a door, a window, a staircase and something that looks like a broom. Vera says it reminds her of the tower of Babel.

I never understood that story.

'Why did God come down and destroy something that seems like a valiant effort?' I asked one night, lying next to Vera in bed. 'All they wanted was unity.'

'God had something better in mind for the people,' said Vera, hand on my chest. 'A new project.'

I kissed her shoulder. 'To be dispersed? Living far from each other and not being able to speak the same language?'

'I like to think that in being forced to reach out to each other we might understand something about love that we otherwise may not have known,' said Vera.

Vera grew up in a Presbyterian home. Her father died when she was five. A couple of years later her mother married Bob, the pastor of a small church.

I like Vera's mother. I like her quiet humour and her kindness, and I like the way she treasures the table of white walnut that I made for her. But most of all I like that she was a good mother to Vera and still is.

Outside the wind pulls at the bare branches and the sky is grey. I finish the last bit of my sandwich and then I see Vera leave the studio. Our home phone rings as I watch her disappear into the garden shed.

'Yes,' I say, as I answer the phone.

'Mate, you didn't ring.' It's Neil on the other end. My brother's voice is distinct and gravelly—street smart and educated at the same time—and always somehow evocative of his freckles and now-greying red hair.

'I haven't spoken to her yet,' I say and watch Vera emerge from the shed with gloves and a pair of shears. She begins to cut the branches of a rosebush and I wonder if it's the right season for it.

'Are you sure this is what you want?' Neil says.

'Is the place vacant or not?' I ask, pulling at the phone cord so I can arrange the kindling in the fireplace as we talk.

'I've already told you it is.'

'Then I'll get back to you later.' I hang up without waiting for him to reply.

The front door slams and Vera appears in the doorway. She is white with cold.

'I was thinking of going for a walk,' she says. 'Do you want to come?'

'Where to?' I ask.

'Down the ravine.'

I consider it. 'It will be dark soon.'

'If we go now it should be fine. It's a clear day.'

We walk down the path, Vera in front. It's the gums that preside over this place. They tower over us. White gums, spotted gums, red gums.

We walk slowly, carefully, watching each step. Everything is dry and cold. And it's getting darker. I regret walking down this late.

Vera picks up some kindling and places it against a tree the way she always does for us to pick up on the way back. Then we continue, further and further down until she stops abruptly in front of me. My heart starts pounding, sure she has come across a snake—but instead it's two kangaroos standing on the path, heads turned towards us, grey coats and fine faces. We watch without saying a word until they disappear into the thicket.

Had it been before Ben disappeared Vera would have looked back at me and said, 'Extraordinary, aren't they?' And she would have taken my hand as we continued further down. But today we walk separately.

Ten minutes later we are almost at the bottom and I follow her across the creek, stepping on the stones we have placed in the stream. And then we are at the waterhole.

The place is like a secret garden of ferns, water and rocks, enclosed by sandstone walls. We come here almost every night during summer. On hot days the waterhole is cool, its muddy water like silk, and when temperatures are at their highest we float on its silvery surface until our skin is wrinkly and pink. Today the waterhole is black and cold. A few weeks ago it had a thin crust of ice, like glass. We had seen the water move beneath it, slow yet animated, as if it held a secret life.

'Neil rang.' My words seem like intruders in the quiet landscape.

'Yes?' she says.

A large lizard sits on a protruding rock on the opposite bank. It looks otherworldly in the fading light.

'His faculty rents out a house to artists and visiting scholars,' I say. 'They have a cancellation.' I feel my heart thump against my throat as I continue, 'I'm considering renting it.'

Now I have said it. Now I can't take it back.

She turns and looks me. 'What do you mean?'

I want to tell her that I am a drowning man, that I can't bear it, I can't bear any of it. But all I manage to say is, 'We can't keep doing this.'

'For how long?'

'It's available for half a year,' I say.

Vera looks out onto the waterhole, and the place is getting colder and darker by the minute. A cockatoo calls out above us, the sound distinct and unnerving.

'Are you leaving me?' She keeps her gaze on the dark water.

'No,' I say and want to take it all back. How could I possibly think it's a good idea to be away from her?

Then she looks as if something had just dawned on her. 'Where is this place?'

I hesitate.

'Where?' she insists.

'In Newtown,' I say, then add, 'I'm not going to look for him.'

She doesn't answer.

I look at her beautiful profile and the long hair that

falls down her back. Her brown jumper is old and worn. Everything about her is familiar. Everything about her is light years away.

She picks up a small rock and throws it hard into the water. It hits the surface with a thud. Deep ripples form.

The lizard on the bank opposite disappears into a crevice in the rock wall. Vera keeps her gaze on the water.

'Please don't go,' she says.

I reach out and touch her arm. 'Let's head back.'

Her eyes fill.

'Vera, it's getting dark.'

She shrugs away from me and begins to undress.

'What are you doing?' I ask.

She places her jumper on the rock next to her, then her shirt.

'Vera, this is crazy. Don't go in the water.'

She kicks off her boots and gets out of her pants and briefs.

'There was frost this morning,' I say and reach for her again. But she walks out onto the rock and dives into the dark water without a word.

The surface settles and is blank like a mirror. I wait, hearing my own breath in the quiet. Another moment goes by. She is not coming up, and I scramble to the edge about to jump in when she appears way out, gasping for air.

I watch her climb up onto the rocks, and then she

stands in front of me. Her hair clings to her body and there are streaks of mud between her breasts.

'He is dead, David.' She speaks slowly, her voice like rust. 'He jumped from the Gap. He either died hitting his head going down or he drowned. Either way he is dead.'

She bends down to put her shoes on.

'You need to get dressed,' I say, and pull off my jumper. 'Use it to dry yourself.'

But she doesn't listen. Instead she bundles up her clothes and walks ahead without waiting for me.

'Vera,' I call out after her.

She keeps walking. Her back and legs are as white as the ghost gums surrounding her. I can hear her crying in that odd coughing way I have become numb to.

I cross the creek as quickly as I can and catch up with her.

'Vera,' I say. 'Please put your clothes on, people could come.'

She turns abruptly and I almost slip, but she doesn't reach out to steady me.

'People?' She spits it out.

I don't know why I said it. I don't care what anyone thinks, of course I don't. But she is gone up the dark path before I can say a word, and soon she is out of sight.

—

I pick up the kindling, and make it out of the bush, almost expecting to see an overturned truck or some other accident caused by Vera's naked appearance. But there is no one around. The air smells of snow and smoke from the pot bellies fired up around the village, and the sky is streaked with ink and blazing red. I wonder if Vera noticed it as she crossed the road and walked down our driveway.

I put the kindling in our woodshed and walk across the courtyard to the house. The door is locked and I can hear the shower going. I sit down on the doorstep and wait. Minutes turn to half an hour, night falls and the moon appears, yellow and full.

When I hear the shower turned off I get up and knock hard on the door. Vera appears with a towel around her and for a moment we stand awkwardly in the narrow hallway between coats, gumboots and fishing rods. Then she takes me by the hand and leads me to our bedroom.

She lets the towel drop to the floor and the sight of her makes me ache. We don't speak, not a word as I fumble to get out of my pants. But before the funeral, even during the time when Ben was missing, there were words, always words, between us. Not necessarily coherent talk, but always a murmuring, a fluidity between daily life and lovemaking. Now there is silence and it's all moving too fast.

'No,' I say, when she pulls me on top of her. 'Not yet.'

'I want you to,' she says, but gasps in pain when I enter her.

'I can't,' I say and feel my whole body shake.

'I want you to,' she says again, but turns her head when I try to kiss her.

And in a mixture of anger and desire I push into her and keep pushing until I collapse on top of her. She gets out from underneath me, picks up the towel from the floor and leaves the room. And then I hear the shower go again.

I am overcome with self-loathing. Outside the moon has lost its yellow glow and has turned the colour of bone. The worst thing has just happened.

I don't know how long I lie there, but some time later I hear the front door slam. Vera has gone back to the studio.

I want to run after her. I want us to find what we seem to have lost: the language that used to be between us, the ordinary weaving into the extraordinary so tightly that there was no distinction. But I've got no idea how to get it back and right now I almost doubt it ever existed. I don't know who we are any longer, I don't know who we are without Ben.

They say he got up one morning and travelled to the Gap, to those mighty harbour cliffs. They say he jumped and that a witness spoke to him just moments before. They say it happened on a summer's day, at a time when everything is blooming and bursting and so full of promise that it breaks the heart right open.

I can't imagine it; I can't imagine him hitting the hard surface of the ocean or, worse, the rocks beneath the cliffs. But I see him in my dreams: Ben in freefall. Sometimes I see him going down head first, sometimes feet first. I see him in midair, shirt fluttering, hair tossed by the wind. And I look into his blue eyes and in that moment, and of this I am sure, he is begging me to find him.

I get tomatoes and an eggplant from the fridge. And then I go back for some of the preserved lemon that I know Vera likes. I feel as if I have been in an accident, a car crash or a random shooting. My hands look pale in the kitchen light as I cut into the eggplant. Some of the purple bleeds into the flesh.

I walk outside to see if the parsley has survived the frost. The light from Vera's studio glows warmly between the trees at the bottom of the garden and I remember how it used to be; how I would take a break from work and walk across the lawn to see her.

She would take me by the hand and show me her work, and I would inhale the sharp smell of welded metal.

'I used copper for this one,' she would say. 'Feel how smooth it is.'

And I would pull up her skirt and realise with joy that she wasn't wearing underwear and that she was wet to my touch.

She would continue, 'I am about to engrave it.'

I would touch her, hearing her breathing quicken.

She would whisper, 'You smell of oil.'

And I would say, 'I'm finishing the table.'

She would reply, 'Your arms,' and moan as she let me enter her against the workbench.

I would slow down, and she would touch the outline of my tattoo: a diver in old-fashioned diving gear, done in an alcohol-fuelled madness the day I walked out of uni. 'You have nice arms,' she would say.

And I would respond. We repeated lines said many times before and each time it was exquisite, each time it was as if it had never been said.

I take a last look at Vera's studio before I walk back inside the kitchen carrying a limp bunch of parsley. And it is only when the rice is ready and the table set that I walk through the dark garden and knock on her door.

She turns in her chair as I walk in. Her reading glasses sit low on her nose and she is holding a metal file in her hand. But her workbench is empty and I can see that she has been crying.

'Vera,' I begin.

She takes off her glasses. 'Don't,' she says and rubs her eyes. 'Please don't say anything.'

I wait outside as she turns off the lights. Through the

glass door I glimpse the shelves behind her, full of tools and random objects. On a corner sits a troll doll with a flame of pink hair. It's been there for years. She bought it for Ben when he turned five, but he never took to it. I understand why, it's terribly ugly, but for some inexplicable reason Vera decided to keep it. When it comes to her creative work there is no telling what might inspire her.

She joins me on the steps and together we walk across the lawn, a dark sea of grass cold against our pants legs.

The tall pines in Rob's garden sway soundlessly and the village smells of frost and dead leaves.

'Vera,' I say into the darkness as we walk.

'You've decided to go,' she says. 'I know.'

I reach out to squeeze her hand, but she won't let me.

I wake in the night and find the space next to me empty. The house is quiet. I get out of bed and find her in the dark living room with the TV on mute. On the screen young men cleave through aquamarine water; swimming caps and elongated bodies.

It's the same every night.

She recorded the video for a project. It was just before Ben went missing and I have never asked her why she is still watching it.

'Vera,' I say. 'Come to bed.'

And without saying anything she gets up and follows

me down the hallway through our old squeaking house. She gets into bed and turns away from me. Not a word is spoken and I fall into a dreamless sleep.

Vera and I don't talk about my upcoming departure over the next couple of days. She disappears into her studio every morning and I work hard on finishing the table, worrying about whether Vera will be okay when I go.

She has always been fiercely independent. Before we met she hitchhiked around South-East Asia for more than a year. On another trip she travelled part of the Silk Road on the back of a camel. There is a photo of her as a nineteen-year-old sitting on the hood of a Land Rover in khaki shorts, a white T-shirt and heavy walking boots, with a string of turquoise stones around her neck. She looks so completely at ease in the desert landscape. She has still got that strength, I know it's there. But now there is a fragility too. I see it in her eyes; she is barely making it through each day.

I continue to sand. Some of the sanding can be done by machine, but most of it needs doing by hand. It takes hours. Slowly, very slowly, the dense grain of the mulberry comes out. The tabletop is thin, so thin that it looks like it's floating.

I apply oil. I prefer Danish oil, but it tends to stain the darker woods, so I use Osmo instead. I lather it into the timber and then let it sit for a couple of minutes before wiping it off. After that I apply the oil again. I do this three times before finishing off with a coat of oil wax.

I stand back and study the table. The grain of the mulberry is beautiful and complex. It was the right decision not to add an inlay.

The table is picked up the evening before I leave. The buyer, a soft-spoken tall man, arrives just before dusk in a rented van. He stands in my workshop with an attitude of reverence. 'I have always wanted to work with wood,' he says.

He explores the grounds while I cover the table in bubble wrap, and I can hear him and Vera chatting in the garden. Their voices drift and fall, and then suddenly, as if by a miracle, Vera laughs. The sound startles me.

'You are a lucky man,' the buyer says as he comes back into the workshop. 'Your wife is full of charm and you have wild apples in your garden.'

When we load the table onto the truck I almost ask him to stay for dinner—just so I can hear Vera laugh again.

I walk back to the workshop after he's gone. The smell of oil and sawdust hangs in the air, but the place feels empty. Ginger is asleep on her mat in the corner and I bend down to give her a pat. She opens her eyes and stretches, and then falls back asleep.

I need to decide what timber to bring to the city in the morning. I know there is a workshop connected to the rented house, but I haven't given any thought to what I might be working on while I'm there. I get the box with my inlay pieces and then go through my shelves of timber. I choose oak and some darker pieces of rosewood and on impulse I walk to the back and drag out the log of spotted gum that has been drying in the corner for years.

The gum had died on our neighbour Rob's property. Ben was living in the city then, but came up with Neil one Saturday to help cut it down. They arrived full of bravado and spent an entire day in Rob's backyard cutting the tree into firewood. I was busy in the workshop, but stopped to have lunch with them. They were laughing and bantering, sweaty in jeans and T-shirts. At that stage Ben had already shut me out, and I was jealous of Neil then, jealous of the easy chatter and the rapport between them. The boy I knew—the boy I taught to ride a bike, joked with, put to bed at night—had without any explanation turned prickly and sullen towards me.

They left that night after dinner. Crammed into Neil's red mini they beeped the horn repeatedly as they went down the driveway. I didn't stay to see them turn the corner.

Vera joined me in the kitchen a moment later. She leaned against the kitchen bench and waited.

'How come they get on so bloody well all of a sudden?'

I said, putting a stack of plates into the cupboard. 'Ben used to think Neil was a pretentious know-it-all.'

'Ben will come back to you.' said Vera. 'And it's good that he's got Neil.'

'But there's no reason for him to shut me out,' I said and closed the cupboard door. 'Did you hear him ask me when exactly I stopped caring for the underprivileged? What does that even mean?'

Vera took my hand and said, 'It's teenage rebellion, darling. It's just come a little late. He never went through that phase, you know.'

I knew Vera was probably right, but I couldn't handle it. I wanted him back. I wanted him to fling his arms around me, rather than giving me a limp handshake as if he were some boarding-school kid and I his estranged dad.

Night has fallen, stars have come out and it's freezing as I load the timber onto the ute. I add the portable bandsaw and most of my handheld tools, and then I cover it all with a tarp and strap it down.

Ginger emerges from the workshop and makes a beeline for me in that slow stiff walk of hers. She rubs against my leg as I look up into the night sky. *Ben*, I think. *If you came home I would gladly have you think I'm an old fool. I would gladly take the rejection just to have you back.*

Vera gets up before me on the morning I am set to leave. The weather has changed. The sky is grey and heavy with a rain. I hear her digging in the garden as I get up. The shovel hits the hard ground again and again, and by the time she comes back in I have made coffee and set the table.

She washes her hands at the sink, then sits down across from me, reaching for a piece of toast.

I push the butter closer to her. 'What are you doing?' I ask.

'What do you mean?'

'In the garden?'

'I'm digging a hole for the rose that I planted down near the studio. I'm going to move it up to the others.' She looks at me, the expression in her grey eyes unreadable.

Before I can ask why she is gardening in the middle of winter she says, 'Tell me again why you're going.'

'Vera,' I say and put my cup down. 'I'm not going to look for Ben, I just don't know what else to do. What happened the other night, it's...'

She looks down at her toast and sadness fills the room. Her flannel shirt is open over a worn black T-shirt. The beauty spot that I have kissed a thousand times sits just above the neckline.

Outside the wind pulls at the long grass, the sky is concrete.

'Come and visit,' I offer, and then feel embarrassed at how it sounds. No invitations have ever been necessary between us. I reach for her, but she stands up and opens the pantry door.

She pulls out a jar of marmalade. It's been there for at least five years and neither of us has ever been tempted to open it.

'You need to terminate Ben's lease,' she says and sits back down.

We've kept the place for Vera's niece, who is eighteen and lanky and dreams of city living the same way someone dreams of marrying a rock star. She's asked us to hold the flat until she gets a deposit together.

'We can afford to give her a bit more time,' I say and watch Vera spread marmalade on her toast.

'She's not going to move, David. It's been five months.'

'Okay, if you're sure. What do you want me to keep from his place?' I ask.

'Nothing.'

'There must be something you want?'

'Give it all to Vinnies.'

Her kiss is brief and hardly felt when we say goodbye. I watch her walk across the lawn to her studio, and I am left to feed Ginger before I leave.

Sydney has two faces. The sparkling coastline with its sandstone cliffs and whitewashed houses where million-aires and surfer-boys with salt-crusted eyelashes view the city as a backdrop to their existence. And the inner city with its poverty, decay, homeless people and wild, restless life. I prefer the latter.

The traffic slows down when I reach Parramatta Road. I pass car-yard sales, boarded-up restaurants and wedding-dress shops that look like they belong to another decade. There is no one on the footpaths; everything is deserted. The buildings are sodden and the clouds hang heavy over the grey skyline.

The house has seen better days. Its yellow facade is peel-ing and the side gate is loose on its hinges and gives a loud squeak as I open it. Neil once described Newtown as having so much charm that no one notices it is falling apart. There is some truth to that. In fact the whole terrace-lined street is dilapidated, but every front yard is bursting with flowers and bushes and the street is lined with paperbark trees.

I knock on the back door as instructed. A pair of old runners has been left near the steps. There is a hula hoop in the long grass and a child-size plastic table near the fence where jasmine descends from the neighbour's backyard like a waterfall.

A dog starts yapping on the other side of the fence, but stops as abruptly as it started. I check my watch. I am just on time. I sit down on the doorstep and inhale the air. Jasmine. This is how Sydney smells in August. I had forgotten.

I stand up a few minutes later when I hear someone at the gate.

'Hi,' says a woman, pulling the gate shut behind her. She has bright red hair, and is out of breath. 'I'm Pat. I'm so sorry for keeping you.'

She looks like a movie star from the fifties in her polka-dot skirt and short white fur coat. Underneath the coat she wears a black AC/DC T-shirt. I like her straight away.

'I'm not usually late.' She searches through her bag and pulls out a set of keys. 'But my daughter was sick at kindergarten and I had to pick her up.'

'Where is she?'

'Who?' She turns sideways and looks at me as she unlocks the door.

'Your daughter?'

'Oh,' Pat walks inside and reaches for the light switch. 'She's with a friend watching *Spider-Man*. She's probably eating something full of sugar as we speak.'

I follow her inside.

Pat draws the curtains and light falls onto a clean

living space with an adjoining kitchenette. 'Do you have any kids?'

'No,' I say.

A worn lounge sits along the wall. Above it hangs a framed Kandinsky poster. It's one of his depictions of Moscow and I have a sudden painful memory of Vera, gloved hands and red cheeks, at Red Square during our honeymoon.

'That's probably a good thing,' says Pat. 'People with kids often decide to leave early.' She turns towards me. 'Neil says you're here to work on some designs. Woodwork?'

'Yes,' I say.

The kitchenette looks basic, but clean. An old percolator sits on the kitchen bench.

Pat follows my gaze. 'We call him Perkie. There's a stack of good coffee in the freezer, all for your consumption.'

I put my bag down.

She walks over and opens the fridge. 'Sorry, I just need to check that everything is in order. Our previous resident left yesterday and we had a cleaner in last night.' She moves on to the cupboards, peering into them one at a time. 'So you're Neil's little brother?'

'Only by a year,' I say. 'But he's quick to point it out.'

She laughs. 'Neil is such a charmer. If I were one of his students I would totally fall in love with him.' She checks the cupboard under the sink. 'The workshop is in there, by the way,' she points to the door on my right. 'Have a look.'

I walk into a white-walled workshop with skylights. It has a good-sized work table and a bench perfect for the bandsaw. At the back of the room there is a metal sink and an empty bookshelf.

'Is it going to work for you?' Pat calls out.

'It's perfect,' I say.

She appears in the doorway. 'Then I'll just show you the upstairs and leave you to it.'

I follow Pat through a door next to the kitchenette and up a set of stairs.

The room faces onto a leafy lane and the back of a small church. It has slanted walls and features a made-up double bed and a desk next to a blue-curtained window. It resembles something between a scout's cabin and a cheap hotel room, but it's clean and has an adjoining bathroom.

'So this is it.' Pat puts her hands on her hips. 'I sometimes come to do some admin, but just close the door to the stairs if you want privacy. I'm quiet when I'm here.' She hands me her card and a set of keys. 'Ring if you have any questions. I live around the corner. My address is on the card.'

The scent of her perfume sits like an itch in the air after she's gone.

I open the window and inhale. The aroma is familiar. It's the smell of people, pleasant and insistent: washing detergent, fuel, garbage bins and a whiff of something spicy frying that makes my stomach growl. I walk back downstairs and unload the ute quickly before walking up to King Street.

People eat at tables outdoors despite the cold. A woman in Doc Martens and a purple shawl drinks tea outside an Indian diner with a scruffy-looking dog sprawled on her lap.

There is movement and colour everywhere I look. King Street attracts artists, students and people living on the streets, and I am met with voices, beards, tattoos, swearwords, hats, skirts, chains, piercings and men begging on the sidewalk.

I decide on the Indian diner and order lamb curry and a lassi so yellow that it seems to emanate light. From the window seat I gaze at the street. Newtown looks different from when I used to live here, but it feels the same.

I rented a room above a butcher's shop after I left uni. It was a dump. The toilet was downstairs and I shared it with the butcher and his two apprentices. They left bloody handprints on the sink and never cleaned. I would wash in the tiny kitchen upstairs or at the local swimming pool if I had money. The place was freezing in winter and suffocating in summer, but the lease allowed me to use the back shed for my woodwork and for that alone it was worth it.

By then my mother was already famous. Her book *Exterior Politics* had become an international bestseller and students flocked to hear her speak.

I brought Vera to one of her lectures. It was held in the quadrangle at Sydney Uni and the hall was packed. Vera and I squeezed in at the back next to the open window and then my mother made her entrance, rushing in with a briefcase under her arm. She didn't know we were there and didn't see us. Applause broke out, brief but enthusiastic.

'Oh,' she said as she reached the front, 'you are being entirely silly and adorable.' And then she put on her reading glasses and began the lecture. I didn't hear a word of what she was saying. I just kept thinking that I too would have clapped had I not known her. There had always been a kind of heat emanating from her. People responded to it, and that day was no exception; that day she made everyone feel that Political Science 101 was a gateway to a brilliantly inspired life.

When the lecture finished the guy next to me said, 'Man, I always feel like I can fly after hearing Bessie speak.'

'Bessie?'

'That's what I call her in my mind,' he said and smiled a crooked smile.

After the lecture I introduced Vera to my mother, who multitasked perfectly. She handed out papers, gave someone a hug, nodded seriously at someone else's comment and still managed to ask Vera all the right questions. What did she like about art school? Who was her favourite sculptor? And she had looked amused when Vera and I joked about the inescapable heat in my room and how we had tried to haul an old bathtub up the stairs. The endeavour had been unsuccessful, the tub too large for the bend in the staircase, and we had ended up bruised and exhausted from our efforts.

'So what do you think of the famous Beatrice Oliver?' I asked, as we walked home.

Vera looked at me sideways. 'She doesn't like you very much,' she said.

Her words hurt me even though they were true.

I shrugged. 'My brother and I don't inspire her. She finds it hard to deal with our mediocrity.'

'What?'

'That's what she once told us.'

Vera was quiet for a moment then said, 'Darling?'

'I know what you're going to say.'

'No,' she said, 'I don't think you do.'

'You're going to say that my mother is a total idiot and that I am far from mediocre.'

She laughed. 'That's true, but I'm not going to waste

my time talking about her. I was going to ask you out for ice cream.'

Then, as always, the exception to the rule. Not long after our visit to Sydney Uni my mother turned up at my doorstep unannounced, carrying a heavy roll of black material.

She pinned the material to the top of the windowpane standing on my only chair while I scrambled through the cupboards in pursuit of a near-empty jar of Nescafé. Filling the kettle I protested, 'It will make it even hotter in here.'

'If the sun doesn't come in, the heat will stay out,' she said, snipping off black material, making it fit the frame.

It proved right. I lived in cool darkness during the day and at night I pulled the curtains aside to let the air in. My dreams were filled with traffic and drunken yelling and my limbs were iridescent and strange looking in the light from the street. One night I woke and caught sight of my foot and in the time it took for me to wake fully I watched it with horror, trying to work out what was moving at the end of my bed.

The material was an aberration; one of the few loving things my mother had done for me. And when winter came I couldn't bring myself to take it down. Besides, it seemed in reverse to keep the place warm. I kept it drawn all the time until Vera woke one morning laughing. 'I can't see a thing,' she said, and then, pretending to be blind, she patted my face, and said, 'You have a wonderful face, young man.'

The spices bring tears to my eyes. The curry is good and I wonder if Ben has eaten here. Chances are that he has. He and Vera are adventurous when it comes to food, adept with chopsticks and connoisseurs of all cuisines. We used to take Ben out whenever we came to the city. We let him choose the place. Often it was Japanese and very expensive.

On one of those occasions we had just picked him up from the airport. He had spent a month in India working on a sanitation project in the desert of Rajasthan. Both Vera and I were surprised when he chose engineering. It had seemed too conservative somehow for his restless idealism. But through his involvement with Engineers Without Borders it had all started to make sense. During dinner he talked about sustainable development and the power of humanitarian engineering with the fervour of a religious fanatic.

'What's new?' Ben had asked me, reaching for a plate with sashimi and glistening roe.

He sat beside Vera, tanned and lanky, wearing a black shirt.

'What's new?' I repeated, preparing myself for what was coming.

'Sold any tables lately?'

'You don't want to hear about my tables,' I said.

'Ben,' Vera said and put a hand on his. 'You've just come home. Let's enjoy this meal without arguing.'

That stopped him momentarily. 'Grandma visited,' he said.

'Visited?' said Vera.

'She came to Jaipur,' he said, picking up a piece of salmon.

Vera looked sideways at me.

'Really?' I said.

Vera poured each of us a glass of warm sake. 'Was it something you had arranged?'

'No, but she was on her way to Europe and made a stopover. They all thought she was really cool.' Ben got his phone out and showed us a picture: my mother in a dark blue sari next to Ben, both beaming at the camera.

'Your grandmother is full of surprises,' I said. But I wasn't really that surprised. My mother pulled stunts for Ben's love. She loved him in a way she never had Neil or me.

'Did you know,' Ben continued, 'that a whole family in India could live ten years on what one of your tables sells for?'

'Ben,' Vera said.

'It's a table, Mum,' he said. 'I'm just saying. Why does it have to be beautiful? Why should people have to pay so much?'

I tried to defend myself even though I knew it was futile. 'Design and art are always worthwhile. Beauty is something that enriches every culture.' I knew I sounded pompous.

'Marx said that art was a commodity of the capitalist system,' he countered. 'There is no such thing as beauty outside a cultural definition.' He looked up and winked at the waitress, who in turn blushed so hard she looked like she had run a hundred-metre sprint.

Once again I resented the time Ben spent with my family, but the ample supply of Marxist arguments was Neil's fault, not my mother's. Ben seemed to spend countless hours in Neil's tiny office at Sydney Uni discussing politics.

Ben turned to me. 'Build something that will help people, man.' And then his mood shifted the way it so often did and his eyes flooded. 'That should be the most important thing.'

'Enough.' Vera picked up a piece of plum-coloured sashimi on her chopsticks and offered it to Ben.

'Mum, the eternal rescuer,' he said, opening his mouth.

'Good?' she asked as he chewed.

'Awesome,' he said and gazed at the waitress again.

'He thinks I am sacrificial.' Vera joked and reached for my hand across the table.

'Aren't you?' said Ben.

She swivelled on her stool and looked at him. I knew that look. It was Vera baring herself, showing that something had hurt her.

He looked at her for a moment, then said, 'Sorry.'

She reached over and ruffled his hair. 'Do you want to taste the shrimp?'

It's lunchtime and the Indian diner is filling up. The room echoes with voices. Two men in their seventies sit down at the table next to me. They get out a chessboard as they wait for their meal. One of them looks over at me and taps his hat. I realise he sees me as a fellow elderly citizen and feel like saying, 'I'm only fifty, for goodness sake.'

I finish my meal and consider stopping by Ben's flat on my way back, but push the thought aside. I am not ready to think about packing up his things just yet. Instead I visit the supermarket and buy bread, butter, cheese, milk and a bag of green apples before heading back.

I take the plane to a piece of rosewood, and then spray it with water in order to see the grain more clearly. It stands out like a drawing. It looks like a man staring out to sea. Turned on its side it could be an aeroplane zooming into a storm. It's too beautiful, too distinct, and even though I am not sure what I want to make yet I am suddenly certain that neither the oak nor the rosewood is right for the project.

I use all my strength to lift the log of spotted gum onto the bench and then I make a diagonal cut. The log opens up. The heartwood is a dark chocolate with a distinctive thin grain and the sapwood very pale. It's almost the same colour as the small ironbark chest I made for Vera not long after we met. I gave it to her knowing that the gift had weight to it; a weight that went beyond what had been said between us thus far. I felt nervous watching her unwrap it on my workbench, but when the wrapping paper fell to the floor she looked at me and said, 'David, this is beautiful. I couldn't have imagined anything like it, but now I don't want to ever be without it.'

I had felt moved and relieved at the same time, and we had ended up making love on the dirty concrete floor. I had to pick splinters out of my hands afterwards.

And now the decision seems easy. I've always wanted to make a larger chest for Ben, but never got around to it.

I take off my jumper and begin by cutting the log into twelve pieces of timber, enough for a good-sized chest.

I measure and then cut each piece to size before I begin planing. The hours pass and the heat from my labour fogs up the windows. I think about Ben. Random memories come and go, but there are moments of stillness too and that has been rare lately.

When night approaches and the skylights turn dark I leave the workshop and bring a sandwich upstairs with me. Eating at the desk I realise that I can see right down to Sydney Park and the airport beyond it.

Normally I would call Vera about now and tell her about the place. I would start by describing the four dark chimneys at Sydney Park—leftover relics from the brickworks factory that once operated there. Then I would paint her a picture of the airport and its runways and towers glittering in gold and red; a feast of light. Vera likes light.

One night during the first year in Mount Wilson I went to see her in the studio. It was the beginning of autumn; the weather had turned cool with crisp nights and spectacular sunsets. I had just finished a table in bloodwood with a walnut inlay. Vera had touched the inlay earlier, tracing it with her fingertips.

I cooked for us that night and it was almost dark by the time I walked across the lawn carrying our dinner. I had made pan-fried fish, salsa and charcoaled capsicums with tender red flesh. I looked through the glass door before walking in. Vera was on the floor, bent over a large acrylic wing in bright yellow. Her hair was up in a ponytail; four months pregnant, she was still slight.

She was working on an installation. Twelve huge acrylic birds in strong colours, lying on their backs, wings stretched out. Each bird had a unique expression. It was unclear whether they were dead or alive. To this day it's still my favourite work of Vera's.

She looked up as I walked in. 'Darling.'

'I made dinner,' I said.

'Give me a minute.'

I arranged the plates on the step outside her studio and sat down. Venus had appeared in the sky, always the forerunner. The bush smelled of gum and soil and ferns and I was happy. We had lived in Mount Wilson for just under a year. There had been no adjustment period; we moved in and started work straight away, and soon after Vera discovered that she was pregnant. We hadn't planned it. I don't think we had ever talked about having a child, but Vera was happy and so was I.

I handed her a plate as she sat down next to me. Then I untied her hair and put my hand through it.

'Tell me again why you're so good at cooking?' She leaned against me.

Night was hanging in the bushes, caught by the trees.

'I just can't help it,' I joked.

And right then a wallaby with a joey in its pouch crashed through the bush into our garden. We sat very still, watching it feed on the grass. But when Vera adjusted the plate on her lap the wallaby disappeared back into the bush.

'Sorry, wallaby,' she whispered.

Above us the sky was turning teal and stars were appearing quickly.

'The Southern Cross is so bright,' I said.

She reached for my hand. 'One day soon our boy will be sitting here with us.'

'Boy?'

'I think it's a boy.' Then she took a deep breath, inhaling the scents of the night. 'I want him to see this light,' she said. 'To see the beauty and the majesty in it all.'

'I want him to be able to make a table,' I said.

She looked at me. 'A table?'

'To be able to use his hands.'

She nodded. 'That's a very useful thing.'

I leaned in and smelled her hair.

'I want him to know right from wrong,' she said. 'And I want him to be as good a cook as you are.' She kissed me on the cheek.

'I want him to feel loved,' I said. 'I want him to never go one day without love. Not like Neil and I did.'

Vera turned serious. 'I want him to be safe,' she added.

I looked at her, then back up at the stars. We were fairy godmothers sprinkling our wishes over our unborn child.

I stare out into the Sydney night. There are no stars visible, only heavy-bellied planes that lift, one after the other, out of the glimmering cityscape.

I leave the window, switch on the light and unpack my travel bag on the bed. Shirts go in the cupboard, everything

[44]

else in drawers. I hang up my one and only suit, which is well on its way to being out of fashion. I hardly ever wear it. The last time was at Vera's exhibition—the last time I saw Ben.

My mother was there too, in a red cheongsam and with her hair up, striking as always. It was her birthday and she spent most of the night charming everyone around her.

There was one moment when Ben and I were left on our own. We stood next to each other in awkward silence, holding a glass of champagne each. He wore his 'Anarchy Rules' T-shirt and was his usual distant self. I asked him what he thought of the exhibition and he said, 'It's cool.' I asked him how school was going and he said, 'Fine.' The only consolation was that surprisingly he treated Neil with the same disdain.

Neil had arrived late, with red-wine breath and a dramatic account of his drive to the gallery. He was wearing a denim shirt a bit too small for him, looking like a fading rock star. The shirt gaped as he spread his arms wide to demonstrate the size of the wombat that had decided to enter the Sydney Harbour tunnel and consequently stalled the traffic for more than an hour. 'It just strolled down between the cars and I rolled down my window and said, "How are you, mate?" And it did this little head shake, you know? From one cool dude to another.' Neil had roared with laughter and then started coughing. The account made me chuckle, but Ben had looked sullen and paid no attention.

My mother circulated over to us and hugged Ben. 'My darling,' she said, 'you made it.'

She gave Neil and me a kiss on the cheek. 'I must confess,' she said, accepting a glass of champagne, 'when I see all these wonderful people I regret not being more adventurous.'

'What do you mean?' I asked, thinking she was plenty adventurous. Probably more so than any of us.

'Look at them,' she said. 'Colourful, that's what they are. They are open to the grandeur of life, to the wide open spaces.'

Neil nodded seriously as if she had just said something incredibly deep.

'And talking about open spaces,' she said, 'I have forgotten to tell you all that I've accepted a teaching position in Arizona. I'm leaving in three weeks.'

'Grandma, that's amazing,' said Ben.

'Isn't it, darling? You need to come and visit, I'll be there for half a year.'

'Ben is just about to start his last semester, he probably won't have time,' I said, and not being able to stop myself I added, 'We are all very proud of him.'

'Please don't,' said Ben.

'There should always be time for some globetrotting,' said my mother, as she put an arm around Ben. 'Maybe we could go out into the desert together. We could sit there for a while, with a few sticks.'

'A few sticks?' I said.

She laughed. 'You know, dry twigs, a circle of stones, like these lovely people here would do. We could even join other like-minded people with twigs and stones of their own.'

'You mean you want to be a hippie,' I said, feeling myself once again charmed by her.

'Maybe I do.'

'It wouldn't work,' I said. 'You would read them the riot act before any twigs and stones were involved.'

'Why?' She looked at me curiously.

Like an experienced soldier I stopped myself. I knew this scenario. I had said something that intrigued her, but ultimately she would be disappointed with my answer. I always fell short. She would up the ante without even knowing it and I would get caught up in an old desire to please her.

Ben was getting ready to go. He put his bag over his shoulder and said, 'Grandma, forget about it. You are a *grand dame*, not a hippie.' Then he hugged her and said, 'Don't forget I'm coming over tomorrow.'

She answered, 'Birthday tea with my grandson, how could I forget?'

I finish unpacking and feel the familiar weight on my chest, a heaviness that feels both wild and dead at the same time. I put my notebook on the bedside table, and then get undressed. Standing under the shower I attempt to cry. I force myself to think of the funeral and the pressure gets worse, but nothing happens. My eyes are so dry they feel itchy.

Getting into bed I glance at the notebook, but I am too tired to sketch. I roll onto my back and stare at the ceiling. The bed linen smells of chlorine and hospital, and I can't help thinking of the time Ben was born.

Vera almost died giving birth to him, but at first we thought everything was fine. It was a winter afternoon, the third of July, when she started having contractions. We left the light on in the bedroom when leaving for the hospital. Vera had made a mobile with horses made out of blue and pink felt. I had crafted a cot out of the lightest shade of ash, with soft corners and smooth polished edges. We had placed it on my side of the bed, because it takes an earthquake to wake Vera. And we had decided on names: Lauren if it was a girl and Ben if it was a boy.

I drove as fast as I could, but had to stop the car three times because of Vera's contractions. Just before we reached Katoomba she said, 'David, don't let them give me any drugs.' Then she added, 'You know what happens to me.'

Once Vera had eaten magic mushrooms at a party in Redfern. Her friends from art school shared a rundown terrace in Abercrombie Street and had arranged an elaborate dress-up party. It had been a feast of creativity. Most people wore masks to go with their outfits and more than a hundred people were crammed into the tiny terrace. There were lions and geese, pirates and mice. One had dressed up as a trumpet, another as Gough Whitlam, and yet another as a plain cardboard box. The standout was the couple who came as the characters in Grant Wood's painting *American Gothic*. The guy even carried a real pitchfork, which became increasingly hazardous as the night wore on. When Vera's hallucinations began the masks came alive. 'David,' she said, clinging to me. 'Their eyes, I swear to you, they're looking at me.' She was desperate to make it stop and having read somewhere that dairy helps counteract the effects of hallucinogens I took her to the corner store to find some. Vera sat down on the footpath in front of the shop and drank a whole litre of milk in one go. Then she looked at me. I had pushed the papier-mâché zebra mask to the back of my head. I liked it a lot; it was the first thing Vera had made for me. But before I knew what was happening she pulled it off my head and stuffed it in the garbage bin next to us.

Passing Katoomba station, window wipers working frantically, I recalled that milk seemed to have absolutely no effect. I had to lead her like a blind person all the way back to Newtown when she realised the hallucinations were triggered by sight.

I overtook a car and saw the emergency sign ahead. 'Almost there,' I said, and glanced over at her. But by then Vera had passed out; her mouth was open and her head dangled against the window. I panicked. Completely panicked. I shouted at her as I leaned forward and sped up the hospital driveway and into the emergency bay. Later, when I moved the car, I saw that there was a pool of blood on the passenger seat.

They were renovating the hospital that day. Jack-hammering shook the waiting room and overshadowed the sounds of monitoring machines.

They brought Ben out to me while Vera was being oper-ated on. I picked him up and held him. He was wrapped in a flannel blanket that felt too big and rough for his small tender body. His face was red and all scrunched up and his eyes were closed, but I could see that he was listening to my voice. I was completely unprepared for the love I felt. Later a nurse appeared and said, 'Your wife will be out soon—they're closing her up now. It all went well.' She had put a comforting hand on my shoulder. 'Do you need anything? Would you like me to take your boy for a little while?'

I shook my head; there was no way I was letting go of him. 'No,' I said. 'Ben and I are fine.'

I fumble with the unfamiliar switch and turn off the light next to me. Streetlight fills the room, and I drift off to sleep. A car passes on the back lane and a dog barks somewhere in the distance.

I wake a little after 2 a.m. A moth, grey as a ghost, bangs against the window, drawn to the streetlight outside. I get up and let it out. It tumbles into the night and is gone in an instant.

The window is still open the next morning and the room is freezing. When I pull it closed I see a priest in a black robe smoking on the back stairs of the church. He has bright red hair and looks peaceful. I can't even begin to imagine what his day might look like.

I check my phone when I get downstairs. There are no messages from Vera, but I am certain that right about now she will be walking across to her studio, carrying a mug of coffee.

The workshop is chilly, but it doesn't come close to the cold mornings in Mount Wilson. I eat a cheese sandwich standing in front of the workbench. The room is dim, but I don't turn the light on. The Japanese masters talk about the importance of waiting for the wood to speak, and I have always found it easier to listen at dawn.

I watch and I wait, and after a little while I see a different way of putting the chest together, one that will bring out the grain and emphasise the depth of the colour. I rearrange the pieces and stand back to have another look. Then I decide to go a bit thinner and I start the day by planing.

The workshop is quiet. Once in a while I hear people pass by on the lane outside, but otherwise all I hear is the sound of the plane. Two hours pass. I move slowly and don't make any quick decisions. I keep turning the wood, I keep touching it.

When I am satisfied with the pieces I begin to work on the dovetail joints. I measure and double check, and then I begin to carve out the joints with chisel and hammer. Wood chips fall to the floor and I work up a sweat.

After another hour I stop for a break. I find the ground coffee in the freezer and rediscover how to use a percolator. As I wait for the coffee to brew I lean against the kitchen bench and admire the framed Kandinsky print in the living area.

Two weeks before we got married Vera was contacted by the Russian embassy in Sydney and offered a solo exhibition at the Moscow State Museum. They had a cancellation and asked if she could fill in the space. I am sure they knew she had spent time studying in East Berlin, but most of all I think it was the article she had written on Russian contemporary art that did the trick.

We had planned to spend our honeymoon in what Neil called his 'romantic fishing cottage' down the south coast. In reality it was a small windswept fibro shack that turned out to be full of asbestos and later had to be pulled down by a white-clad team who looked like a bomb squad. Instead Vera and I booked two tickets to Moscow. Neil was wildly jealous, seeing himself as the only true red in the family.

Vera worked day and night to finish the installation. We had to take out a loan to afford the vast amounts of bronze she needed, but the end result was worth it. The sight of the Giacometti-inspired trees, very tall and very thin, was intrinsically sad for reasons I still can't fathom.

During the exhibition we asked a museum official to translate the poster next to the entrance. It appeared that Vera, without knowing it, had created 'A salute to the victorious and unbroken Russian regime.'

During our time in Moscow we were accompanied wherever we went by three men in fur hats and heavy overcoats. For our protection, they said, but I am fairly certain it was to protect the Russian people from any bourgeois ideologies that might have trickled out of us had we been given the chance to engage in conversation. I still think they must have been just a tiny bit disappointed by our lack of political agenda.

One morning while it was still dark we made our way to the Kremlin. It was snowing and our 'three friends', as Vera called them, were following behind us. The glow of their cigarettes bobbed like lanterns on a string.

Standing knee-deep in snow in front of the Kremlin it was hard to imagine summer in Sydney. A few slow-moving Škodas passed by, but otherwise it was too early for anyone to be out.

We were giddy with excitement; neither of us had seen snow before, but it was more than that. The political landscape was changing everywhere and, even though we didn't know what was coming, we felt we were standing on the brink of something new, something bigger than us. Two days after we returned to Sydney the Berlin Wall fell.

The coffee finishes brewing and I bring it with me to the workshop. But instead of continuing with the dovetails I decide to ring Vera. I get my phone and walk out into the windswept backyard.

'Vera,' I say, as she picks up.

'Yes.'

'Are you in the studio?' I ask and try not to picture her in front of an empty workbench.

'Yes.'

I shiver in my shirtsleeves. The jasmine on the fence is

being pulled and pushed by the wind.

'Neil called last night,' she adds.

'Yes?' I say.

'He told me you're having dinner together.'

I have completely forgotten tonight's arrangement with Neil.

'Maria is making lamb,' says Vera.

I can't bear the polite way we speak to each other. It's much worse on the phone, much worse when I can't see her and at least assure myself that she is still there with me.

Then, in an instant, the wind slams the back door shut. I feel for the keys in my pocket, but know already that I haven't got them with me.

'Vera?' I say.

'What?'

'I've locked myself out.'

She laughs just a little. 'Oh, no.'

'I was going to describe the jasmine for you,' I say, feeling strangely brave in my stranded position.

'You were?'

'It's white and dark pink,' I pause, 'and there are so many flowers it looks like...it looks like the sea when the wind blows on it.'

I feel like I am reading some obscure love poem out loud. I can hear Vera clear her throat. A black bird lands on the children's table next to me. It slides on the plastic and takes off again.

'I'm coming to the city tomorrow afternoon,' she says. 'I have a meeting at the gallery. Do you want a visit afterwards? We could have dinner.'

'Why don't you stay the night?' I say, feeling like I am asking her on a first date.

She doesn't answer, just says softly, 'I'll see you tomorrow.' Then she hangs up.

I feel encouraged. She had laughed, just. And she is coming to see me. I put the phone in my pocket and inspect the house. I know that I won't be able to break my way in. The downstairs windows have bars on them and even if I hauled the plastic table across the yard I wouldn't be able to reach the first floor. I remember the card Pat gave me, still in my back pocket.

I dial her number and notice my phone is almost out of battery.

'Hello,' a girl answers.

'Hi,' I say. 'Could I speak to your mum, please?'

'Who are you?' she asks.

'I am staying in the house your Mum looks after,' I say. 'Could you run and get her, please?'

'I've lost a tooth.' She says it slowly as if she is trying to understand the mystery of losing teeth as she speaks.

'I'll you what,' I restrain myself from raising my voice, 'you get your mum, okay? And then I want to hear all about your tooth.'

'Okay,' she says and then I hear her shout, 'Muuum, there's a man who wants to talk to you.'

I hear Pat's voice coming towards the phone. 'A man?' she asks.

'Yes, and he wants to hear about my tooth, Mum.'

'Hello?'

'It's David,' I say. 'David Oliver. I locked myself out. I'm standing in the courtyard and my phone is almost out of battery. Would you be able to come and let me in, please?'

Ten minutes later Pat walks through the courtyard, holding the hand of a young girl in a yellow raincoat.

'Oh,' says Pat when she sees me in shirtsleeves. 'You poor thing.'

The girl looks up at me. She's the spitting image of her mother.

'Have you got your key upstairs?' Pat unlocks the door.

I nod.

'This is Eloise, by the way,' says Pat. 'She's home from school again today, although she is not really sick any more, are you, baby?'

'Mum,' says Eloise, 'the man wants to hear about my tooth.'

'Not now, darling,' says Pat and lets me in before her.

I put coffee on for a second time while Eloise and Pat go to buy cake. I pull out some sheets of paper from my sketchbook for Eloise and place two pillows on a chair for her the way I used to do for Ben.

They return with a cake in a box. Eloise flashes me a demonstrative smile, revealing a big gap between her front teeth.

'It's from the bakery down the road,' says Pat. 'They make cakes that look like fairy gardens.' She lifts the lid and shows me a cake with candied lemon, purple flowers and shaved coconut.

Eloise gets out of her coat. She is wearing a pink skirt and an orange cardigan. 'We should sing happy birthday, Mum,' she says as Pat lifts her onto the pillows.

'It's pretty obvious we don't buy cake that often, isn't it?' Pat sits down and turns to Eloise. 'We can sing,' she says, 'but it's no one's birthday and I don't have a candle.'

'Doesn't matter,' says Eloise.

'What do you want to sing?' I ask.

'"Bumblebee Is Lost",' she says.

'You might be on your own there.' Pat turns to me. 'Do you know any bumblebee songs?'

'No,' I say, 'I'm afraid not.'

'Doesn't matter,' Eloise says, 'be quiet.' She sits for a

moment with a look of deep concentration on her face.

We wait. Pat raises her eyebrows at me.

Then Eloise starts singing in a loud voice, 'Bumblebee, bumblebee, where are you? Where are youuu?' She looks at her mum and nods.

'Finished?' asks Pat.

'Yes,' says Eloise.

'That was a pretty song,' I say, as Pat cuts into the cake. Eloise nods.

'So,' says Pat, putting a piece of cake on Eloise's plate, 'it's your second day in the Palace.'

'The Palace?'

'That's what we call it.'

'Fitting.'

She chuckles. 'We think so.'

Eloise attacks the cake.

'Do you take milk?' I ask Pat.

'Only if you've got it, I can drink it black.'

I get milk from the fridge and she puts up her hair with an elastic band, revealing a tattoo of a blue and green hummingbird on the back of her neck.

'You are as colourful as your daughter,' I say and put the milk next to her.

'I should hope so.' She smiles, then glances through the door to the workshop. 'Have you always worked with wood?'

'Pretty much,' I say. 'And you? Are you an artist?'

'I finished a degree in accountancy last year. I work part time at the faculty looking after their admin,' she says and puts a hand on Eloise's back. 'Slow down, Pumpkin, there is plenty to go.' She looks at me. 'You seem surprised?'

'I am,' I admit.

'I just love numbers,' she says. 'It was love at first sight when I was introduced to the times tables at school.'

Eloise pushes her plate to the centre of the table and says, 'I want to draw.'

'You can use the paper next to you,' I say.

'The big ones?' she asks hopefully.

'Yes, but I'm afraid I've only got pencils,' I say.

Pat opens her bag and puts a box of crayons in front of Eloise. She winks at me. 'Let's just say black is not her favourite colour. Give it ten years and it will be all she likes.'

'I want to draw a chimney, Mum,' says Eloise.

'Good, darling,' says Pat, then turns to me. 'Eloise is obsessed with the chimneys down at Sydney Park. I read *Rapunzel* to her the other day and now she is convinced there is a princess living in each of the chimneys, all waiting to be rescued.'

'There are four chimneys, Mum. One, two, three, four.' Eloise keeps drawing. 'And four princesses.'

'She likes to count too,' Pat says. 'Do you know that

new water reserve they have down at Sydney Park?'

'No,' I say and take a bite of the cake. It's creamy and tart.

'It's attracted so many birds. It's just beautiful. But we had to stop visiting, because every time we went Eloise tried to count them all. It was a source of much grief, because they keep moving.' Pat laughs. 'So unfortunately we're missing out on the only wildlife nearby, but you live in the mountains?' She leans over, adjusts Eloise on the chair and then gives her a kiss on the cheek.

'Yes,' I say and notice how naturally Eloise receives Pat's love. Just like Ben did as a boy.

'I used to have a boyfriend in Blackheath,' says Pat. 'He lived in a caravan, can you believe it? Crazy artist. Every day he would get up and paint the sky. He did it religiously. Eloise was little then. She and I would get in my car and drive up on the weekends.'

I get out of my chair to fetch the coffee pot and pour more for both of us.

'One morning,' Pat continues, 'I woke up and it had snowed during the night. It had built up on the window ledge, completely covering it, and for a moment I thought the whole caravan was under snow. But there was this light pushing through the snow and it was the most beautiful light I've ever seen. I'll never forget it.'

'Did I see it?' Eloise lifts her head from her drawing.

'No,' says Pat. 'You were sleeping.'

'But I remember it.'

'You do?'

Eloise turns back to her drawing, her face full of concentration.

'She doesn't,' says Pat and she looks at me. 'She was barely two and sound asleep.'

Pat is beautiful. There is both a wildness and an earthiness to her. I can hear her breathe between the words and sentences.

I look at Eloise. She is leaning over the paper with a purple crayon in her hand.

'What are you drawing?' I ask.

She puts the crayon down with a theatrical sigh as if she constantly has to deal with adults asking about her creative process.

'It's a chimney,' she says.

'Right.' I stand up to get a better look.

'And this,' she sighs again, 'is you.' She points to a stick figure standing in the window of the chimney.

'Me?' I ask, moving closer.

'Mum says that you don't have to explain your drawings,' says Eloise.

Pat looks amused. 'Don't let her boss you around.'

'I am all for it,' I say. 'It's never too early to set artistic boundaries.'

The house turns quiet when they leave. A ray of sun stumbles randomly into the room. It brushes over the leftover cake and lingers on Eloise's drawing. I look at the stick figure in the window of the chimney. She has given me a black moustache and long golden hair that falls to the ground in wavy locks. Next to the chimney it says 'David Oliver' in crooked letters. Pat had turned in the doorway as they were leaving and said, 'Sorry about the hair.'

It's early afternoon by the time I get back to work. I recheck the measurements of the remaining dovetail joints and begin to carve, slowly and carefully, step by step. A millimetre off and it won't work.

I stay in the workshop for a long time. The light changes from dark to grey. Suddenly a burst of sun breaks through the skylights. I stop work and stretch, and before I continue with the joints I fetch Eloise's drawing and tape it to the wall. She reminds me of Ben, headstrong and full of imagination. Although Ben had a fragile side to him as well.

During his third year at Blackheath Primary School we were called in for a meeting. School was out and Ben was playing football in the windy schoolyard with the other kids waiting to be picked up.

Vera and I were seated in Ben's classroom, ready to meet his teacher. The sun fell brightly on the tabletops, twenty squares lit up, and the room smelled of varnish and packed lunch boxes.

Ben came up and knocked on the window. He was chewing a red frog and flashed us a big smile. 'Ben, no way,' Vera said, and went to the window. But by the time she wrestled it open he had already taken off and joined the other boys, shirt untucked.

She sat back down next to me, 'Really?' she said. 'Red frogs? He should know better than that.'

'You're beautiful when you're mad,' I said and leaned over to kiss her. My tongue found the corner of her mouth and she opened it. One of us moaned just as Ben's teacher walked in. She stopped short in the door and we jumped apart.

'Sorry,' I said.

She was young, in a brown skirt and practical shoes, and was blushing just a bit as she sat down in front of us.

'Nothing to be sorry about,' she said and placed a folder on the table between us.

Despite her youth she had a quiet authority and I understood why Ben liked her.

'Ben,' she started, 'is creative and full of energy. And I like him very much.' She played with the edge of the folder. 'The other day I asked the class what they want to be when they grow up. Most said things like wanting to become a vet or a firefighter, but Ben announced that he wanted to be the first person to go to Mars.'

'Mars?' I said. 'That's ambition for you.'

The teacher nodded. 'Ben is certain, though, that a girl will get there first. He said, "Everyone knows that girls are 'sipeerious' at reading maps."'

Vera laughed in that loud uninhibited way that I really like.

'I have absolutely no sense of direction,' she said. 'I can walk down the street and get lost. But David can find his way anywhere. You could drop him in the middle of the bush without a compass and he would find his way home.'

'Like a labrador,' I say.

Vera chuckles, then looks at the teacher. 'So for the sake of keeping some kind of dignity I need to assert regularly that my map-reading skills are superior to David's, or maybe I should say "sipeerious" from now on.'

The teacher smoothed her skirt and looked at us. 'Ben is funny and full of great ideas,' she said, 'and he is not afraid to speak up. But he's also sensitive, too sensitive at times. I found him crying in the bathroom the other day.'

'Crying?' Vera leaned forwards.

I instinctively looked out into the yard and spotted Ben chasing the ball with a small group of boys.

'It's not the first time I've found him crying,' said the teacher. 'And every time he seems unable to tell me what's wrong. That's why I wanted to speak to you today. Is everything all right at home?'

'Yes,' said Vera and reached for my hand. 'Yes, he's really happy at home.'

'That's what he told me too,' said the teacher. 'But we are concerned that he isn't able to explain what's going on. I thought it might be helpful for him to see the school counsellor.'

I continue working on the dovetail joints, remembering how Vera and I had said no to the offer of counselling. Ben told us on the way home that he had fallen during recess and that was why he had been crying. It seemed to be a misunderstanding, and neither of us thought to press the issue. The boy we knew was happy and everything seemed fine.

Now I can't stop thinking about those moments, the moments when we might have failed him or overlooked something. I sift through our life together for clues, for any kind of explanation as to what might have caused him to get up one morning and leave everything behind.

I keep working, slowly and methodically, and by the time I have completed the third piece of timber I feel tired, almost jetlagged. I regret organising dinner with Neil, and on the spur of the moment I decide to walk to Sydney Uni to see if I can catch him. If I stay for a cup of tea he might give me a pass on dinner.

Sydney Uni is a maze of old and new buildings. Being the oldest university in Sydney the campus has evolved over time like a European city, haphazardly, a new building here, a new road there. It's impossible to walk through it in a straight line.

I lived in a college dorm on campus for a year and remember it clearly: the shared kitchen, the drafty study halls and the rooms that smelled of sweat and hormones.

Ben didn't want to live on campus when he started his degree. Instead he found a small flat in Newtown and asked if Vera and I would pay for it. We said yes. We could afford it and I think we were both secretly relieved that he hadn't decided to join a rock band or go on a never-ending surfing trip.

There is another moment I keep returning to. It happened the day before Ben moved out. It's the last time I remember us being close. He came to see me in the workshop wearing his usual jeans and black T-shirt. He was indisputably good looking, and just that morning Vera had said, 'He is becoming as handsome as his dad. I foresee broken hearts all over Newtown.'

'Have you finished packing?' I said and stopped the bandsaw.

'Yeah.'

I took off the goggles and put them on the workbench. 'I could do with a break. Do you want a beer?'

'No,' he said. 'And Dad, you don't have to do that.'

'Do what?'

'Be the progressive dad, you know.'

I felt a bit hurt. 'I'm not trying to be anything.'

'No one else gets offered a beer by their dad,' he said.

'You're eighteen, aren't you? I know you drink at parties.' I put the ruler back in my pocket.

Ben came over and touched the table. 'Cherry?' he asked.

'Yes.'

'It's nice.' And then he looked up at me, eyes brimming with tears.

'Ben?' I walked around the table and put a hand on his shoulder. 'What's going on?'

He fell into my arms, his whole body shaking with violent sobs, his tears soaking my work shirt.

'Ben,' I said. 'Ben, it's okay.'

But he kept crying, and all I could do was hold him.

When he finally stopped he looked up at me with red eyes. He was about to say something when I reached behind me for a box of tissues.

I handed him the box. 'What were you going to say?'

'Don't worry, Dad,' he said, his voice hoarse from

crying. And he went back to the house.

Later I went and knocked on his door. I could hear him practising the chords to 'Space Oddity'. And not for the first time I marvelled at how good he was at everything he put his mind to.

He was sitting on the floor with his guitar. Everything but the bed was packed into boxes and ready to go.

'Do you want to talk?' I asked.

'I'm fine.' He kept strumming.

I waited.

He looked up at me. 'Don't worry, Dad, I'm fine.'

I didn't press. Instead I went to see Vera in her studio to work out what we were having for dinner.

Now it haunts me. Now I keep asking myself if everything would have been different had I listened to him instead of reaching for that box of tissues.

The next morning we helped Ben load the small rental truck. His futon weighed half a ton and was impossible to carry, and there were two lamps, endless boxes of books, bed linen, pillows and a box of brand-new crockery that Vera had bought for him. There wasn't enough space in the truck. No matter how hard we tried we couldn't fit in the old armchair and promised instead to bring it to him the following weekend.

Vera cried as Ben drove down the driveway.

We went back inside and stood for a moment in the

living room uncertain about what to do next. The house was quiet. Tiny dust particles hung in the light. Then Vera took my hand and led me to the red lounge. She had paid a fortune to get it upholstered—keeping, I am sure, the old upholstery shop in Katoomba going for at least another year.

On the red cover of lilies and hummingbirds she lifted her dress and gently eased herself down on top of me. She sat with closed eyes, breathing slowly, and I studied her; studied her eyelids, her mouth and her perfectly shaped nose. And then she opened her eyes and let me in, and everything else fell aside and all I wanted was her.

Once again the house became an extension of our intimate life. We made love in the kitchen, against the desk and on the cool floor of the laundry next to the washing machine on an insanely hot summer's afternoon. Our intimacy spread and unfolded and those years were some of the most productive we both had.

It's mid-break. A few people sit on the old quadrangle lawn, but otherwise the majestic building with its tall spires and maze of stairways is empty.

I am out of breath when I reach Neil's office on the third floor. I can hear Dizzy Gillespie playing inside.

'Neil,' I say and knock on the door.

He appears behind me, carrying a mug of tea. 'Mate,' he says, 'what are you doing here?'

He is wearing a shirt in some tie-dyed pattern. His curly hair is in a ponytail and he wears a brown rubber band around his wrist, the kind that Ben used to wear, showing solidarity with some cause or other.

'Have you got time for a break?' I ask.

'Of course.' Neil opens the door and lets me into his cramped office. His desk is overflowing with papers. 'It's been one hell of a semester,' he says and puts his mug on the desk. Then he opens the window. 'Maria tells me not to smoke in here.' He shrugs and lights a cigarette and stays next to the window. 'She says that I'll end up burning the place down, but you know...' He gestures to the mug. 'You can have my tea,' he says.

'Thanks.' I sit down and reach for the mug.

Posters cover every wall. There is a bit of everything. One promotes a music festival in Munich and features a host of large-breasted women. Next to that is a black-and-white print of Camus, his hair swept back, cigarette dangling from his mouth. There are posters waging war against funding cuts and inequality, and one of Angelina Jolie as Lara Croft, Tomb Raider. It's one part sex and three parts revolution.

'How's the house?' Neil leans against the windowsill and cool air rustles the pile of essays on his desk.

'It's okay,' I say.

'Pat is gorgeous, isn't she?' He takes a drag on the

cigarette and blows the smoke out the window. 'Not politically correct, I know.'

'When have you ever been politically correct?'

'That's true,' he says, looking cheeky as ever. 'Why start now?'

It has started to show that he drinks too much. His face is puffy and there are small broken veins on his nose.

'How was Jared's birthday?' I ask.

Neil pauses, then taps the cigarette out the window. 'It was good.'

'You decided not to have family over?' I say, still feeling hurt that Vera and I hadn't been invited, even though I'm sure neither of us could have coped with a kid's birthday party.

'We just had a few of his friends over, you know?' Neil sends me an apologetic look. 'They spent the whole day collecting ants in the garden, by the way. No need for party games.'

Vera had bought an ant farm for Jared. It sat on our kitchen table for two days. Neither of us could bear looking at it and I was relieved when she finally took it to the post office.

Neil stubs out the cigarette and closes the window. 'Vera rang last night. She's pissed at me.' He sits down across from me. 'She said you've come here to search for Ben.'

'What did you tell her?'

'That you're here to heal.' He picks up a pen and taps the pile of essays in front of him. 'She is a feisty lady.'

'Why?' I ask. 'What did she say?'

'She told me to cut the psychology bollocks.'

My chair is rickety and I half-suspect that Neil has left it like this on purpose. I imagine a little song and dance between him and his students, all ending in Neil offering them his chair. My big brother has always needed to be liked.

Neil continues, 'I've never told you, but there was one time when I thought I saw him too. I was leaving work late one night. It was right after the funeral. I walked out of the quadrangle and down the main stairs when I saw someone who looked just like him. My heart literally skipped.'

I sit up in the chair. 'Did you get close to him? Did you check?'

Neil looks as if he feels sorry for me. 'David,' he says, 'I knew straight away it wasn't him. It was just a moment, you know? Losing someone messes with your head.'

'You think I'm mad?'

He reaches for the mug and drinks the dregs. Then he strolls back to the window. 'I think DNA testing is reliable. I think Ben is dead.'

It sounds rehearsed. I'm sure he's been waiting for a chance to throw that one at me.

'Well, I need to get back,' I say. 'And about tonight...'

He shakes his head, knowing what I am about to say. 'Please, don't cancel, mate. Maria has been cooking all morning.'

I hesitate.

Neil pushes the window wide open and lights another cigarette. I wonder how many he smokes a day.

'I just spoke to her,' says Neil. 'She's in the middle of baking a cake.'

'All right,' I say and get up. 'Then I suppose I will see you tonight.'

'David, before you go...'

I wait, hand on the door handle.

'I know you don't want to hear this, but Mum has come home. I picked her up from the airport last night. She wants to see you.'

'Right,' I say. 'No word from her for four months and now she wants to see me.'

'I think she's sorry.'

'Neil, she is not sorry and you know it. I don't want to see her.' The air from the hallway is chilly.

'She's tanned,' says Neil. 'The department lent her a yellow Mustang with a sunroof, can you believe it?' He looks down at his cigarette. 'David, something's not quite right with her.'

'You're right about that.'

'No,' he looks up at me. 'There's something else. I can't

put my finger on it. Except that she's started to forget things.'

I wait.

'She forgot Jared's name at the airport. And when I carried her luggage into the house she said, "The cats need feeding right away." And I said, "Do you mean the pigeons?" And she turned to me and she looked scared, she looked really scared.'

'I can't help you, Neil. But I will see you tonight, I promise.'

'Bring a couple of reds,' he shouts after me as I walk down the carpeted hallway.

I attempt to take a shortcut across campus and get lost. So much for having a great sense of direction. Trying to orient myself I realise that the School of Engineering is right in front of me.

Two young men are leaving the building, one wearing a T-shirt, the other in a black coat. They part ways at the corner.

How long before I realise? How long before I recognise his walk and the green canvas backpack with the Che Guevara patch?

A minute, maybe two?

Then I begin to run. 'Ben,' I shout, 'Ben!'

A group of workmen in vests and hardhats turn and look at me. Everything stands in relief as I run: the leaves on the pavement, the sun skimming the red-tiled roof ahead, and the smell of cigarettes and Nescafé. I run fast, but when I reach the corner he is gone. I continue down the empty street, past closed faculties and empty bike racks. Everything is quiet. I pull at doors, one after the other, and yell his name into vacant stairwells. But there is no one around.

There is an oval at the end of the street. A young man in a striped jersey is running the track.

'Hey,' I shout. 'Please, hey!'

He comes to a halt, his jersey soaked with sweat.

'Did you see someone walk by just a moment ago? A young man your age, wearing a black coat.'

The runner shakes his head.

'His name is Ben,' I say. 'Curly hair. Tall.'

'No,' says the runner as he takes off again. 'Sorry.'

Then I do the only thing I can think of: I hurry back to the engineering building and knock hard on the locked entrance door.

A window on the first floor is flung open and a young woman in a grey beanie looks down at me. 'Hi,' she says. Her nose sounds blocked.

'I just saw a man come out of this building,' I say. 'Did you see him?'

'Was he wearing a T-shirt?'

'No,' I say.

'That's Tom, the idiot,' she says. 'It's ten degrees outside and he's in a T-shirt so we can see how much he works out.'

'There was someone else,' I say. 'A man. Dark curly hair, black coat. He has a green backpack with a Che Guevara patch.'

'Do you know Tom?'

'No,' I say. 'It wasn't Tom.' My skin prickles with pins and needles and I feel like I am about to throw up.

'It sounds like you know him.'

'There was another boy...man.' I correct myself. I try to talk as slowly and patiently as I can. 'He was walking out with Tom just a moment ago. He is my son, his name is Ben.'

'Your son?'

'Ben Oliver. He's enrolled in the engineering program.'

She shakes her head. 'There was no one here but Tom and me.'

I head for Ben's flat on shaky legs. The traffic along King Street is dense and smoky. An old truck comes to a squeaky halt at the lights. I glance up at the driver. A clumsy attempt has been made to transform his cabin into a home. The curtain to the sleeping area behind him is held to the side by a red string. A plastic garland hangs on the rear-view mirror and a thermos rests on the dashboard. I am immediately certain that this man has no one in his life—that no one cares about where he is and what he's doing. I see my future self in him. And I know that without Vera I will be floundering, that without her I will be completely lost. And because of that I head back to the house instead of going to Ben's flat.

Back in the house I walk upstairs and sit down on the bed, feeling as if I have narrowly avoided a catastrophe. I reach for the notebook on the bedside table. If I am not going to search for him then at least I have to document what I saw. I write: 'Ben 2.30 p.m. Electrical engineering, Sydney University.'

As soon as I write the words they feel like a betrayal.

Vera cried for weeks after the funeral. She kept asking, 'How could this happen?' And I kept saying, 'I don't know, Vera. I don't know.'

All we knew was that a woman who wanted to remain anonymous had spoken to a young man at the Gap that matched Ben's description. He had seemed agitated and had been pacing near the edge of the cliffs. The woman returned to her car and phoned the police. With them on the line she had walked back to the cliffs, but by then the man was gone.

I couldn't bear hearing Vera cry. A cloud so big, so enormous, had descended upon us and it felt as if we weren't going to make it through. I was in a daze and no matter how many painkillers I took I had a constant headache. Three weeks after the funeral I asked Vera's mum to come and stay with Vera while I went to the city. I spent the whole morning searching Ben's place again. I went through his books, his papers, his computer, but found nothing, not even the tiniest clue as to what might have happened to him.

I headed home early that afternoon. And then, driving down a sun-drenched King Street, I saw Ben's lanky frame walk into a pub. I parked in the middle of a bus zone. I was sure, I was very, very sure. I even went as far as thinking that Ben needed to come home and stay with us for a while so that we could all recover from what had happened. What a comedy, I thought, running across the street. What a gigantic mistake.

The pub was near empty and scorching hot despite the ceiling fans. A few people were sitting at the bar, a couple on stools facing the street. The place smelled of beer and piss. Two women in their sixties sat in front of the poker machines in matching nylon dresses, their bags tucked at the side of their stools.

I ran to the back of the pub, into the kitchen and then out onto the back lane, but he wasn't there. Then I searched the bathrooms.

A man in his twenties, a younger version of Neil with bright red hair and a striped shirt, was smoking a joint at the sink.

I glanced at the cubicles. He followed my look.

'Are you a spy, bro?' he asked.

'No,' I said.

'You're one of them spies,' he insisted.

'I am not a spy,' I said and felt like punching him.

'Want a puff?'

'No, thank you.'

'No, thank you,' he mimicked.

I could hear him laugh as I left the bathroom and walked out of the pub.

On the drive back to the mountains my certainty grew. I replayed the image of Ben walking into the pub as I raced past cliffs and gums; the dry landscape seemed infused with hope, bursting with wild beauty.

After parking in our driveway I rushed into the house and barely managed a hello to Vera's mum, who was in the laundry pulling clothes out of the dryer. I found Vera in the kitchen. She was pouring water into the coffee plunger and I took notice of the steam hitting the window glass. Vera was wearing a sleeveless blue dress. Her arms were tanned and her feet were bare in her work boots. Her hair hung loose, reaching her lower back.

'Vera,' I said. 'Something just happened.'

'What?' She turned towards me, her eyes red and swollen from crying.

And the words fell out of me. 'I saw him. Just now.

Vera, Ben is alive.' And then it was out—hot, hard and irreversible.

She looked at me. The kitchen was quiet. I couldn't read her.

Then she turned her back to me.

'I saw him, Vera.'

The border collie two doors down gave a whine, something in between a bark and howl. The light moved, flickering with the tree outside, and licked the hem of her dress.

'Vera? Did you hear what I said?'

'Don't.' She stayed with her back towards me. She reached out and picked up a rubber band from the bench. It was purple. It came from a bunch of asparagus that we had bought the day before. She put up her hair, slowly.

'Vera,' I said and took a step towards her. The floorboards squeaked and I had a sudden image of being in a war hospital talking to someone badly injured. 'Vera,' I said, 'we don't know for sure. We don't know that he's dead.'

She grabbed the full coffee plunger and threw it to the floor; it shattered into a thousand pieces and coffee was everywhere. On her, on me.

Then her legs gave way and she slid down against the kitchen cupboard until she sat on the floor. She started to cry.

Her mum appeared in the doorway holding a pair of my workpants.

'Vera.' I bent down to help her up. 'Vera, don't sit on the floor, there's glass. Don't.'

She didn't hear me. She kept crying and when I placed a hand on her arm to help her up she scrambled away from me, past her mum and out of the kitchen. I could hear her enter the bathroom and the shower being turned on.

The glass fragments glimmered in the light like stars. I thought for a moment that that was how it was going to be from then on; that somehow I had broken something bigger and that the kitchen would forever be inhabited by coffee grinds and tiny shards of glass.

We didn't talk about it. Vera avoided me for days and none of our movements were in sync. One night several weeks later I found her in the living room watching the video of the swimming races again. I turned the TV off and together we walked through the dark house. She didn't turn away from me when we were back in bed. I moved closer, put a hand on her back and drew her towards me.

'No,' she said, stiffening against me. 'Don't.'

I waited for her to say more, thinking how different her voice sounded. Still deep, still warm, but frail somehow.

'Grief,' she said into the darkness. 'Grief does different

things to people. What you experienced...seeing Ben, it's grief, David. It's nothing but grief.'

I reached out and took her hand.

'But promise me,' she said, her voice catching, 'promise me you'll stop this. Ben is dead. He will never come back to us, David. This is it—you and me. This is all there is now.'

I put the notebook back on the bedside table and I lie down. I pull the covers over me and with the wind rattling the windowpane I doze off. I sleep for what feels like hours, deep and undisturbed. But just before I wake I dream of Ben. He is falling through the air. And in the dream I feel the rush of wind and the weight of his fall. I hear him call out for me and wake myself up by shouting, 'I will find you, Ben. I will find you.'

I sit up in bed, my heart beating unbearably fast. It's almost dark outside and it has started to rain. Then I remember dinner with Neil and stumble into the shower.

It's completely dark by the time I walk up to King Street. Sheets of rain lash onto the footpath and the rush-hour traffic is slow. I buy three bottles of red wine from a bottle shop and wish I had brought an umbrella with me.

～

The bus is packed. Next to me a woman is checking her phone; no one is talking. The rain hammers against the windows and I am almost lulled back to sleep.

When I get off in Leichhardt the rain has stopped. Norton Street is busy. People are doing their last bit of shopping and I can't help it. Before I turn into Neil's street I quickly scan the crowd for Ben, but he is not there.

The bottles clink in the plastic bag as I walk to Neil and Maria's single-storey house at the end of the road. Neil bought the house, two streets away from our mother, when he was in his mid-twenties. I thought then that he was destined to stay a bachelor forever. He liked women, and as far as I could tell they liked him too. But he never seemed interested in something more permanent. In retrospect I should have picked up on the signs. He spent two years renovating the house inside and out. He painted the walls and restored the floorboards; he even built a brand-new kitchen despite the fact that he doesn't like to cook. I think he was preparing for a family and that he somehow knew Maria and Jared would come along one day.

Vera and I first met Maria eight years ago. We came to visit Neil, but it was Maria who greeted us. She opened the door wearing an apron with small red hearts on it, the strings wrapped twice around her tiny waist. An Italian beauty with a lavish smile and jet-black hair. Neil hadn't told us anything about her and for a moment we thought it was the wrong house. Later we learned that she had already moved in.

Neil beamed at us all night, as if he wanted to shout, 'Isn't she just wonderful, isn't she just perfect,' and we nodded in silent agreement.

That evening Maria insisted on seeing a photo of Ben. I showed her the one in my wallet: Ben as a four-year-old sitting on the floor in a ray of sunlight with a book in his lap.

'What is he reading?' asked Maria.

'A picture book called *Once I Had a Plane*,' said Vera. 'It was his favourite.'

Putting the photo back in my wallet I joked that Ben had grown just a bit since then and that he, as a matter of fact, was in the middle of hosting a party in our absence. Before leaving for the city Vera and I had made sure to stow away three paintings, some of Vera's favourite glasses and our Alvar Aalto vase.

Maria turned to Neil and said, 'Promise me that we are going to have a child like this?'

I watched Neil reach for her hand and in that moment I saw his life unfold in a way I could never have predicted.

Tonight Maria greets me at the door once more. I can smell lamb and rosemary as I give her a hug.

'I don't think I have ever seen you in black,' I say and notice how pale she is.

Neil appears from the living room. 'Little brother,' he booms and puts an arm around my shoulder.

'Will I be able to get out of here?' I joke, seeing Maria slot two security chains into place.

'We had a break-in last week,' says Neil and he leads the way to the living room. Maria disappears into the kitchen.

The dining table is set. Tea lights flicker in glasses. The table was a wedding present from Vera and me, made of ebony to match Maria's piano. It has a star-shaped inlay in its centre.

I hand Neil the bottles.

He inspects the labels. 'Good choice, bro,' he says.

'A break-in?' I ask, as I sit at the table.

Neil unscrews all three bottles, then pulls out a chair and sits across from me. He lowers his voice, pouring us each a glass. 'We had a man walk into the house. Maria surprised him and then he left. End of story. But she's not taking it well. I've put an extra lock on the door, but she can't seem to get past it. Please don't bring it up. Let's have a good time together,' he says. 'We all need it.'

Maria appears with a tray of sliced lamb on a mountain of roasted vegetables. 'What do we need?' She puts the tray down.

Neil puts an arm around her. 'Time together,' he says.

'And that takes three bottles?' she asks.

'They need to breathe, baby. We can always put the caps back on,' says Neil.

I look at Maria and wonder if Neil has actually noticed how much her appearance has changed. She looks like she hasn't slept in weeks.

'Please start, David,' she says. 'I'll be right back.'

'Where's Jared?' I ask and help myself before passing the tray to my brother.

'He fell asleep about an hour ago,' says Neil.

I catch a glimpse of the red slippery dip in the backyard as I help myself to the food.

Maria returns with a bowl of string beans.

'Jared had Little League this afternoon,' she says and sits down.

'He's still playing baseball?'

'Yes,' says Maria. 'He's good too.'

Neil sends her a warning look.

She throws up her hands. 'What? For goodness sake, Neil. Surely we're allowed to talk about Jared.'

Neil doesn't look at her. Instead he lifts his glass and drinks.

'The food is delicious,' I say. And it's true. Maria has always been a great cook.

Then we make small talk. It's mostly just Neil and me doing the talking. We discuss the advantages of living in the city versus the country. We talk about the introduction of creative courses into universities and whether or not it is appropriate. We talk about Shaggy, my mate from uni, who became a surfer instead of an academic. And we drink. We don't mention Ben or why I am staying in the city. And all the while Maria is quiet. Something is not right, but I don't know how to address it.

Neil pours more wine.

Maria shakes her head when he leans over to pour her another glass. 'Any more and I won't be able to get us dessert.' She collects the plates, then leaves the living room.

I stand up.

'She doesn't want help,' says Neil.

'I'm going to ask her anyway,' I say and wonder when he became so old-fashioned.

I carry the tray across the hall, but stop short in the kitchen doorway. Maria is leaning against the bench. Her eyes are closed. Something in her body has gone loose. The apron that made her look so capable just a moment ago suddenly looks like an abandoned prop. Her breathing is shallow, her face is flushed, and I wonder for a moment if this is what she looks like when she makes love. I am about to leave when she opens her eyes. They are full of fear. 'David?' she says.

'Are you all right?' I step closer.

'Yes.' She takes a deep breath, then turns and puts the stacked plates into the empty sink. She reaches for the kettle and fills it. 'Did you want coffee or tea?'

I search for another way of asking her what's going on, but nothing comes to mind. 'Coffee, please,' I say.

Something is obviously wrong. And Maria never wears black—she is fond of colour. I remember her wearing a bright blue dress at Ben's funeral. Later she told me that Ben once said the colour reminded him of an old video that Vera and I used to watch. I knew immediately which one he meant. It was the one with Jacques Cousteau diving into that great blue hole off the coast of Belize.

Maria gets dessert forks from the drawer and opens the fridge. 'How's Vera?' she asks, pulling out an iced chocolate cake.

'Okay,' I say.

She looks at me. 'What you two are going through is harder than words can describe.'

She says it with such empathy that my eyes fill.

Then we hear music from the living room. The Ramones are belting out 'Can't Get You Outta My Mind'.

'Three bottles of wine,' we say in unison, sharing an old joke. I attempt a laugh, but Maria only gives me a hint of a smile.

The chocolate cake and red wine are a perfect match. I am eating a second slice and am well on my way to getting drunk. Neil puts the album on again from the beginning and dances his way over to the bookshelf to get his pipe. He still moves the way he did when he was younger: a kind of jerky march on the spot reminiscent of Ian Curtis. He has always been so assured in his belief that he is a good dancer that he almost pulls it off. He sways as he lights his pipe.

Neil is probably the last intellectual in Sydney who believes that smoking a pipe enhances his image. Slowly the living room fills with the smell of pipe tobacco, oddly reminding me of the pigeon manure in our mother's bird shed.

Pipe in hand Neil dances to the table and reaches for Maria.

'Come on, darling,' he says, 'dance with me.'

Maria shakes her head.

'You are the light of my life,' he belts out, making up his own lyrics, 'you are the queen of my existence.'

I shake my head. I'm not the only one who's drunk.

'Neil, let go,' says Maria.

He clumsily caresses her cheek before sitting. 'I almost got a smile out of you,' he says.

Then Jared appears in the doorway wearing his Thomas the Tank Engine pyjamas and my heart begins to pound. He has grown since I last saw him. His blond hair catches the light and for a moment I am filled with wild jealousy. I want Ben back. I want my life back, my perfect, ordinary life.

Jared rubs his eyes as he walks into Maria's arms. 'Why are you so loud?'

'We are just talking,' says Maria. 'Uncle David is here.' She kisses the top of his head.

'Off to bed, Jared,' says Neil and glances at me.

Jared looks at me from across the table, then he walks around and leans into me, his body sleepy and warm. He reaches out and touches my watch.

'Uncle David,' he says.

I put a careful arm around him and feel that I am about to burst into tears. 'How are you, buddy? Are you okay?'

He nods. 'Did you bring a present?'

'No,' I say. 'I'm sorry.'

'That's all right.' He looks up at me, cheeks flushed with sleep.

Maria walks around the table. 'Uncle David got you the ant farm, remember?'

He nods as she leads him away from the table.

'I want some cake,' he says.

'It's a cake for adults, you wouldn't like it.'

He absently takes her hand and follows her towards the door. 'I would,' he says.

'Trust me, darling. Come on back to bed. Wave goodnight to Uncle David.'

'Goodnight.' He turns and waves, then follows Maria out of the room.

Their voices fade as they walk down the hallway. I think of Ben and the dream I had just before leaving the house. I am well on my way to getting drunk, but even in my stupor I see it clearly. It makes no sense to keep my promise to Vera if Ben is still alive. It makes no sense at all. I've been crazy to not check his flat.

Neil gets up and turns the music down. 'Sorry,' he says without looking at me.

I swig the remaining wine in my glass. 'What are you sorry for?' I ask.

'Don't be like that,' says Neil.

'It's always good to see Jared,' I say in the most sincere voice I can muster. I look at the cake on the table and suddenly the mixture of wine and cake doesn't sit well. I put my glass down and stand up. 'I'm going,' I say, making sure I've got my keys.

'Don't go, mate,' says Neil. 'I have some scotch somewhere. Let's finish the night on a high.'

Maria comes back in. 'He's asleep already.' She looks at me. 'Are you leaving?'

Neil gets to his feet. 'Stay and have another drink. Come on, mate.'

'I've got things to do,' I say. I walk into the hallway and get my coat.

Neil follows me. 'Tonight? It's almost one in the morning.'

'Just let me go,' I say and reach for my scarf.

'We didn't get to talk about Mum,' says Neil.

'I've already said I don't want to see her.' I fumble with the lock.

'David,' he says, I don't know if I can do it without you.'

'Do what?' I ask.

'Her,' he says. 'I don't know if I can deal with her on my own.'

I give Maria a kiss and pat Neil on the arm. 'See you, mate, get some sleep.'

I open the front door. The cold air is a smack in the face.

Norton Street is pitiful late at night. The Italian restaurants with their green, white and red signs look seedy. The garbage bins overflow and mist hovers in the park across the road. I wait at the bus stop. I wait for ages, but the street is deserted.

A plastic bag is picked up by the wind. It rolls like a tumbleweed across the street and into the dimly lit park.

Just as I consider walking back to Newtown a taxi rounds the corner. I climb into the back seat and give him Ben's address. The driver has the radio on. Sinatra's 'My

Way' booms through the speakers as we race past dark terraces and apartment blocks. I start to feel queasy, and the driver throws me a steely look in the rear-view mirror.

'I'm all right,' I say.

We cross Parramatta Road and continue up Church Street. It has started to drizzle and the abandoned streets are shiny in the streetlights. We pass a lit-up sandstone church and then a deserted car park and a moment later we come to a halt in front of Ben's building.

I give the driver a fifty-dollar note and tell him to keep the change. I stand in front of the red-brick apartment block.

I hold the door for a young woman in rain gear with a blonde ponytail. She pauses in the doorway, looking as if she wants to ask me a question. But the nausea has returned and I don't stop. Instead I unsteadily climb the two flights of stairs to Ben's flat.

Once inside I lean against the door and wait for my stomach to settle. In the darkness I see the contours of Ben's bed and the ancient fridge that he bought at a garage sale. Outside the balcony doors it continues to drizzle and mist clings to the dull streetlights.

I flick on the light.

Nothing seems to have changed since the last time I was here. Ben's guitar leans against the wall next to his bed and Karl Marx still looks at me sternly from a poster on the wall. The kitchen bench is clean and so is the mahogany table that I made for Ben before he left home.

I open the desk drawers and go through them. I continue my search in the cupboards and the fridge. Nothing has been touched; everything looks the way it did the day Vera and I drove to the city to look for him.

That day the place had been hot and stuffy. A full bowl of Weet-Bix sat abandoned on the bench top. It was mouldy and smelled sour.

Vera had stared at the bowl. 'Something is not right, David,' she said. 'Something has happened.'

We went through drawers, cupboards and bookshelves searching for a clue to where Ben might have gone. In between a pile of textbooks I found his old picture book *Once I Had a Plane*. The cover shows a small boy in a checked shirt and cowboy hat standing with legs spread on the wing of a crop duster, cheeks rosy and hair butter yellow. For the first time since that morning fear swept through me.

I went out onto the balcony and tried once more to get hold of my mother. By that stage we had spoken to everyone else. No one had seen or heard from Ben all week.

She finally picked up.

'He was visiting me the day after Vera's exhibition,' she said. 'He was fine. As a matter of fact he was in a great mood.'

'Have you heard from him since then?'

'No,' she said. 'But he's coming over tomorrow. We're going for a coastal walk. You know, Bondi to Coogee, past the old graveyard. Look, David, you're not going through his things, are you? He's not going to like that.'

'I know my own son,' I said. 'And right now our concerns override any sensitivity he might have.'

When I went back inside I found Vera crying at the computer.

'Did you find something?' I said.

She shook her head.

'Vera.'

'No,' she said, 'don't talk. Let's just go through everything again. There must be something here that can tell us where he is.'

Later we walked around the streets of Newtown looking for him. We didn't speak. The sun was setting as we went through Camperdown Park. Dogs were playing on the grass area, their owners chatting in small groups. The tall gums cast elongated shadows on the green. We ended up near the playground.

'We should check it,' said Vera and gestured towards the playground. 'Just in case.'

The suggestion was absurd. Surely someone would have found Ben if he was lying hurt in a playground. But I followed Vera through the low gate and just as we stood amid the swings and climbing equipment the park lights went on. Vera crouched and started crying again.

I tried to comfort her. 'There's bound to be a good explanation. People don't just disappear,' I said, as much to myself as to her.

Vera kept crying. 'David,' she said, 'I have the most terrible feeling. I think he's gone.'

A man with a small boy opened the gate to the playground. Seeing Vera on the ground made him change his mind. As they walked away the boy said, 'What's that lady doing, Dad?'

I had an absurd desire to call them back, to involve them. Everything suddenly felt too big for us to carry alone.

There was no one in the reception as we walked into the police station.

Vera went up to the desk and called out, 'Hello?'

A constable came over. He was in his thirties, with tired eyes and the bleached hair of a surfer. He was a younger version of my friend Shaggy.

'Yes?' he said.

'Our son,' I said, then had to clear my voice. 'Our son is...'

'Missing,' said Vera.

'We think he is missing,' I added.

'He was supposed to start uni last week,' said Vera. 'I spoke to the faculty, he hasn't been to classes.'

The constable reached for a pen. 'What's your son's name?'

'Ben Oliver.'

The constable wrote it down. 'Age?'

'Twenty-three.'

'Date of birth?'

I gave him the date.

'And the address?'

I gave it to him, while glancing at the grey filing cabinets behind him. How many unsolved cases did they contain?

'Does he live by himself?'

'Yes,' said Vera.

'And when did you last speak to him?'

'Ten days ago,' I said, and thought of the mouldy Weet-Bix on his kitchen bench.

'We're going to stay at his place until he comes back,' said Vera.

Half an hour later we were ready to leave. By then the constable had been joined by a sergeant. We had supplied them with a photo and Ben's bank account details. And we had listed contact numbers for his three friends in the mountains as well as for our family dentist in Springwood.

We walked back out into the hot summer evening and standing outside the police station Vera opened the pamphlet we had been given from the missing persons unit. She took one look at the long list of phone numbers and names of support services, then spun around and walked back inside.

The sergeant was still finishing our paperwork.

'Please,' she said to him, 'please find my son.'

The sergeant put his pen down. 'Ma'am,' he said, 'people go missing all the time, and for all sorts of reasons. Normally it's just a trip somewhere, something spontaneous.'

'Ben wouldn't leave without telling us. He never has. We talk.'

'I'm sure you do,' said the sergeant. 'But I can give you more than a hundred examples of parents coming in here saying the exact same thing. They think the worst has happened and then a couple of days later their son or daughter turns up.'

We felt better after that. Much better. We had heard the voice of reason and our frantic search just moments before now seemed a silly overreaction.

'More than a hundred examples,' Vera said, shaking her head as we walked to King Street. 'Those crazy kids. The things they put us through.'

We bought some takeaway Thai food and took it back to Ben's place. The curries were sweet and tangy and, comforted by the sergeant's words, we chatted during dinner.

'Remember how he once talked about working on a mango plantation?' said Vera.

'He needs a break,' I nodded.

'The surfboard is gone, did you notice?'

'He's been studying hard, got a high distinction the last time we spoke to him, remember?'

But later that night our conversation shifted: 'Maybe he's had an accident—leaving like that isn't like him.'

We couldn't sleep even though we tried. Now I think that we both somehow thought that if we slept it would prove that everything was not as bad as it seemed.

The police knocked on the door at four in the morning.

A body had been found in the ocean two days earlier. A fisherman had caught it in his net. And with our information the dentist confirmed a match.

'I want to see him,' said Vera. 'I want to make sure it's my boy.'

'He's too far gone,' one of the constables said. 'He was in the ocean for more than a week, and at this time of year...'

All I could think about was our dentist, Mr Thompson.

'Our dentist is old,' I said. 'He could have made a mistake.'

One of the officers said, 'We will be running a DNA test, but, sir, we have the dental X-rays. There is no mistake.

We're very sorry for your loss.'

Standing alone in Ben's quiet flat I still don't believe it. I would feel it if he were dead. I know I would.

I find a glass in Ben's cupboard and pour myself some water. Despite the cold I feel like I'm burning up. I open the balcony door. Fog has fallen over the city and muted the traffic noises.

It's only when I'm about to close the door that I see a ceramic gnome with a bright green hat on the floor of the balcony. It has big sad eyes like the dwarves in the cartoon version of *Snow White*. Did I check the balcony last time I was here? I can't remember. I'm almost certain that I would have opened the door to let some air in, but did I actually walk out onto the balcony?

I bring the gnome inside and put it on the table.

Who has been in Ben's flat? Besides the fact that there has never been a gnome on his balcony it's hardly his style. He was never into kitsch and he never went for colour. He always wore black, except for one time a couple of years ago when Vera and I picked him up for dinner.

'But darling,' Vera had said as he opened the door for us. She didn't finish the sentence, but instead leaned in to kiss him on the cheek. During dinner neither Vera nor I mentioned the pink shirt he was wearing, but we spent the entire trip home talking about it.

'It's the colour of the roses at the back of the garden,' said Vera as we were driving.

And she was right. Ben's shirt was made of pink cotton with white stitching, matching the exact colour of our roses.

'He must be helplessly in love,' she chuckled. 'Do you think we should ask him who it is?'

The time when Ben would confide in me was long over and I had no hope it would ever return. 'No,' I said. 'He'll tell us when he's ready.'

I check that the shirt is still in the cupboard. Holding it close to my chest I turn off the light and walk over to Ben's bed. I lie down with the shirt next to me. It has turned pale in the darkness. Night has drawn the colour out of it. I pull the doona cover over me without bothering to take off my shoes. Then I lie still, hand on the shirt sleeve, and stare at the dark ceiling.

Later the police showed us the pair of black jeans that Ben had supposedly been wearing. They were the right size, but otherwise nondescript, and neither of us recognised them. And then, after a week, the DNA results came through.

The body was cremated. Only Vera and I were present. We didn't speak. I held her hand while she cried. A few days later we drove back home. The ashes sat in a small cardboard box between Vera's legs. My driving was jerky.

At one stage I lost control of the wheel and swerved into the grass onto the side of the road, but Vera didn't seem to notice.

When we got home I went into the kitchen and made a plate of food for us to share. My hands were shaking as I cut the bread and I couldn't think of what to get from the fridge. I walked back and forth from the kitchen to the living room so many times I lost count. I kept thinking of things I could add to the table. Vera had put a CD on and started to light a fire despite it being a warm summer's night.

Outside stars were emerging.

'Springsteen?' I asked.

'It' cold, don't you think?' She wiped her hands on her pants. 'It won't be long.' She bent down to adjust a larger log so the kindling could breathe. When she stood back up she almost lost her balance.

I am not the only one, I thought. I am not the only one who doesn't know my body any longer.

'I don't know,' she said. 'Springsteen seemed right.'

'He didn't like Springsteen,' I said, looking at all the food I had put on the table.

'No, but I like him,' she said. 'And so do you.'

I nodded.

'And it's us here, now.' She stood at the fireplace looking at me as if she didn't know what to do next.

I walked over and took her hand and we started

swaying to 'Born in the USA'. It was more of a hanging onto each other than actual dancing, but for some reason it was a beautiful moment, a good moment.

We held the funeral in our garden a week later. Vera wore a green skirt and purple gumboots. It had been raining for days, heavy tropical summer rain. We dragged our long kitchen table out onto the lawn. I had covered the legs with plastic bags, wearing work boots and my suit.

'Are you sure you want this?' I asked Vera. 'We could have it inside.'

She stood, white as a ghost, rubbing her arms.

'He didn't really like the garden,' I said.

'I can't bear being inside,' she said. 'I don't want this memory in the house. Everything else about him, but not this.'

We carried plates to the table and platters with roasted vegetables and five slow-roasted chickens that we bought from a neighbour. There were bowls of crème fraîche, green leaves with dressing, jars of honey, cold butter and bread rolls. I had baked the rolls that morning before dawn. Kneading the dough in the quiet kitchen I had still expected him to arrive home, to walk into the kitchen and tell me that it was all a mistake.

The gums swayed, the oaks groaned and, standing in front of the table, I realised that the spread was reminiscent of our wedding feast in the same garden. We had re-created it without realising.

People started to arrive. Vera's mum and her husband, Bob, who had promised to say a few words. He shook my hand with a formality that was normally never present between us. But his watery blue eyes were kind and offered me a moment of solace. Then a cousin came, and a friend, and then another friend. My mother arrived with Neil and Maria. I never asked where Jared was that day, but I was grateful he didn't come. People were wearing light shirts and summer dresses, everyone but me, strictly following Vera's wish for us all to wear something colourful.

Everyone helped themselves to the food and chatted politely, and it was only after a little while that I realised my mother wasn't in the yard. I went to look for her. The sounds from the garden followed me inside. It wasn't a happy sound, nor was it sad; it was the sound of people trying to be present and polite and at that moment I thought decorum wasn't such a bad thing. Sometimes the air needs to be filled with the sound of good will. Sometimes it's all we have.

I found her in the living room.

'Mum,' I said. 'We're starting now.'

She didn't look at me, just shook her head and began to cry.

I wanted to comfort her, but the early morning, the baking of the rolls, the setting up and the sheer effort of being present had taken everything out of me. 'Please,' I said. 'Could you please do this for me? Mum? I need you out there.'

'Why would he do this to me? Why?' she sobbed.

I stood there wishing I never had to see her again. Then I left the room.

Outside people were wiping hands on serviettes, taking last swigs of red wine, before forming a sombre circle around the large oak where we had decided to bury the ashes.

I should have dug the hole before they arrived. I thought it was going to be easy after all the rain, but instead the soil had turned to clay. I dug and dug. My suit felt too tight and I was sweating in the cold air. No one moved, no one spoke. The sky hung dark and heavy and I could hear my own laboured breathing. It felt like the digging would never end, but finally the hole was deep enough. Vera bent down and put the box into it. She used her hands to push the soil on top of it. She left a handful of dirt and looked at me. 'Do you want to?' she asked, eyes red, cheeks blotchy. I shook my head. She pushed the last bit of soil on top of the box and patted it with her hand. And then she started crying helplessly.

Vera's mum kneeled next to Vera and embraced her. Bob came forwards to speak. I just stood there, holding onto the shovel, wishing I could run into the bush and disappear for good.

Bob said, 'I am not a man of big words. All I will say today is that it's a day of mourning and that my heart is heavy. I am going to read a psalm and then I will pray.'

I remember the words from the psalm: 'Therefore we will not fear, though the earth give way and the mountains fall into the heart of the sea, though its waters roar and foam and the mountains quake with their surging.' The words fell in strange and awkward shapes; they fell on me and into me, and I was surprised how soothing they were.

When Bob finished people started to leave. Some came over to say goodbye, others just nodded at me as they left. I was still holding the shovel and Vera continued to cry.

My mother didn't say goodbye, but Neil hugged me and said with a broken voice, 'Anything you need, anything at all and you ring me.' And I nodded into his shirt, thinking that he smelled of thyme and red wine and that I might never feel happy again. He let me go and looked at me. His curly mane of hair caught the bleak light and for a moment I thought he looked like a prince, like something out of Narnia.

Ben's apartment is quiet; the whole building is quiet. Time passes through me, moving in waves from past to present. Before and after. Vera, Ben and me. I watch the night become brittle. The liquid morning touches the room and

Ben's shirt turns pink again. I bring a sleeve to my face and inhale. And in a supernatural effort, like an experienced perfumer, I separate the smells: one part cupboard, one part winter, one part Sydney traffic that must have snuck in through the crevices of the flat and one part—of this I am sure—Ben. I single that part out and inhale deeply and then I fall asleep.

I wake in the afternoon feeling hung-over. It's drizzling again. Light moves on the white wall, dances across the face of Karl Marx. The place is freezing. I climb out of bed, head pounding, and find my phone. There are two texts from Vera. The first says, 'Coming in this afternoon at 4.30. See you after the meeting. Dinner?' The next was sent half an hour later: 'Meeting postponed, but already on train. Pick me up at the station? x.'

We rarely text and she might not have meant anything by signing off with a kiss. But hope is reckless. It flings itself from skyscrapers and does wild acrobatics with just the slightest bit of encouragement. Right now, despite my hangover headache, I glimpse a life ahead with her. I ignore the gnome on the table and try not to think about seeing Ben. Right now I want to be with her, nothing else.

I empty Ben's mailbox before I leave. There's a birthday card from the local video shop and a bunch of flyers despite Ben's 'no junk mail' sticker. My head is threatening to explode as I drop it all in the garbage bin behind the apartment block. On the single clothes line hang odd socks, T-shirts and a pair of underpants with the elastic gone.

Back in the house I quickly make coffee and bring it with me into the bathroom. I take two painkillers, brush my teeth, shave and shower. Then I down the coffee and get dressed. At the last minute I pick some jasmine and put it in a glass on the desk.

Pigeons have taken over Central Station. They are everywhere: inside, outside, sitting on the rafters, the benches and on the empty tables in the cafeteria. I think of my mother and her pigeons and how she still rents a van every year and travels to Merimbula to set them free. As children we went with her; an excruciatingly long drive in the company of twenty or more pigeons cooing and fluttering in the back. We would see them take flight from a car park near the beach only to drive all the way back home to wait for them. I never understood it, never saw the point of it.

I see Vera at the turnstile and walk towards her. Her long hair is loose and she is wearing her old leather jacket. I remember her buying it early on in our marriage, but I didn't know she still had it. There is a sleep mark on her cheek.

'You slept?' I lean in to kiss her.

She nods. 'You look like you have too.' She lets me

take her bag.

'It got late last night.'

'With Maria and Neil?'

'We drank too much,' I say. 'Are you okay to walk back? It's not far.'

'I know where Newtown is,' she says.

'Of course.'

We walk down the hill towards George Street. It's already rush hour. The sun is setting quickly over the rooftops and the traffic surges and presses along the four lanes.

'Did Maria cook lamb?'

I nod and feel a remnant of the hangover thinking about the meal.

'And Jared?' she asks. 'How is he?'

'He was in bed by the time I got there,' I say.

'You didn't get to see him?'

'No,' I say, and spare her the details of Jared in his Thomas the Tank Engine PJs.

The footpath is busy and Vera walks slightly ahead of me. Lights begin to appear in houses and buildings. The city is turning into one large sparkling creature.

What would I think if I saw her now for the first time? I would think she was gorgeous. Even in the old leather jacket and worn jeans, I would notice her immediately. I know it.

Her hair is tugged by the wind. It touches my arm and without thinking I reach for a strand.

'Ouch,' she says.

'Sorry.' I let the hair go.

'Why are you pulling my hair?'

'It touched me first,' I say and smile.

Then she smiles back and I stand before her, knowing the way I have always known that there is nowhere else to go but to her. I step closer and put my arms around her. My hand finds her back under the shirt and her skin is soft and warm. I pull her to the side, out of the steady stream of pedestrians, and bump into a young man wearing a beanie.

'Careful, old man,' he says as he swerves around us. Someone swears and I don't know if it is at us, but I don't care, because now I have her, I have the language. I know exactly who I am and who she is, all that in the wake of a strand of hair.

'You,' I say and sit down on a brick wall. She follows onto my lap. 'I miss you,' I say against her cheek. 'The city. It's...'

'Big?' she suggests. 'Big and lonesome?'

I laugh. 'It's big and you're not here.'

She pulls back and looks at me. 'Take me out for dinner somewhere. I forgot to eat lunch.'

The diner is crowded, but we order and find a table right

at the back. It wobbles; Vera folds her serviette and puts it under one leg.

'Better,' she says.

The food comes in a matter of minutes and I realise how hungry I am. Naan bread, chickpeas, spinach with cottage cheese. Eggplant and tomato and beef curry. We have ordered too much, but it doesn't matter.

For a while we eat without talking. Then Vera says, 'I've started a new project.'

'You have?'

'Yes,' she says. 'And the house is still standing.'

The joke is old and worn, but I welcome it. We both know that when Vera works she turns inwards. The floors remain unswept and the leaves gather up outside on the stone patio. And I know that without me at home the kitchen sink will fill with plates and cups and dirty knives and tea bags. When she is in the middle of a project there seems to be a force field in her and around her, a thickened state of consciousness. Everything becomes about the senses and in the past, before Ben disappeared, she would make love as if she were trying it out for the first time.

'What are you working on?' I ask.

'I'm making houses,' she says. 'Tiny houses out of tin. Hundreds of them.'

I touch her hand as she speaks, trace her fingers from knuckle to fingertip. Her hands are full of scars from her work. Thin and white, like cotton thread.

'You've never used tin before.'

'It's the most unpretentious of all metals,' she says. 'Cans: baked beans, tomato soup, sardines.'

'You use cans?'

'No, I'm just saying. It comes in sheets. I got a delivery the day you left. The delivery guy looked like he had never been out of Sydney. "You live here?" he asked as if it were inconceivable.'

'Was there anyone around?' I ask.

'Around?'

'Was Rob home?'

'He was harmless.' She puts a hand on mine. 'Don't worry.'

I lift her hand and hold it against my cheek for a moment. 'So, tin?' I say.

'It's soft, too soft really,' she says. 'But the fragility is what makes the project interesting.'

Maybe it's because we are here—here in the city where it all started. Suddenly it's easy to talk. There are no awkward silences between us. We eat too much while talking about the time we met and the butcher's workshop where I used to live.

'You didn't think it would last between us,' I say.

'I thought you were too handsome for it to last. Women

seemed to like you a lot.'

I smile. We have told each other the same story many times before.

She sips her lassi. 'And you had never thought of settling down.'

'That's true,' I say. 'Not until I met you.'

'Even then you were doubtful.'

'Men are slower,' I say.

The words between us sit like archaeological excavations; they dig into our past and reveal what used to be. And I want her. I want the past back. I look down at our empty plates. 'Do you want anything else?' I ask, hoping she will say no.

She shakes her head and I am grateful, not for the first time, that Vera hasn't got a sweet tooth.

Curry burns pleasantly in my mouth as we weave, hand in hand, out of the busy diner. When we reach the door someone else is already seated at our table.

I lead her down a lane and away from King Street. It's almost dark. The back streets are filled with soft dusk. The branches of fig trees reach over the street like canopies.

'I don't remember Newtown being this quiet,' says Vera.

'It's busier down at Ben's end,' I say and hold my breath, knowing that I've spoken in the present, but Vera doesn't seem to mind. She keeps her hand in mine as we cross the same small park I walked through earlier. People are out with their dogs, chattering companionably in small groups. Someone calls out, 'Feeble, Feeble,' and a dog with a flashing light attached to its collar bounds past us.

'Feeble?' Vera whispers. 'Is that the dog's name?'

We start to giggle like two teenagers and I pull her close to me and we rest against the side of a figtree. Its branches are like night arms, full of shadows, full of protection. I reach under her shirt. She isn't wearing a bra. Vera. My hand finds a nipple. I don't care about anyone passing or the fact that we are just around the corner from my place. I touch her and hear her breathe faster. She is mine. I bend down to kiss her.

She stops me. 'How close are you from here?'

'Two minutes,' I say.

'Come.'

Vera smiles a little when I unlock the door and let her walk past me into the living area.

'It's almost like your old bachelor pad,' she says.

I nod.

'Apart from that terrible table, of course. You were so good already then.'

I show her the workshop.

She sees Eloise's drawing on the wall. 'And who did that?'

'The daughter of the woman who runs this place. It's

supposed to be me in the tower.'

'Enviable locks you got,' she says. She touches the timber laid out on the work table. 'What are you working on?'

'A chest. Like the one I gave you. It's the spotted gum from Rob's backyard.'

Her eyes well. 'Ben did such a great job that day. He looked so strong, remember?'

I take her hand and lead her up the stairs, afraid to say or do something that will break whatever is good and right between us now.

I don't turn the light on and Vera puts her bag down and walks to the window and takes in the view as I hoped she would.

'You can see all the way to the airport,' she says.

I walk up behind her and put my arms around her waist.

She pulls out of my embrace. 'I need to get back early tomorrow morning,' she says. 'I didn't plan on staying.'

'That's okay. I'll wake you early.'

'What way?' she asks.

'What do you mean?'

'West, east?' She nods at the window. 'What way are we facing?'

'We're facing south.'

She leans her head on my arm. 'How do you know

these things?'

'Logic.'

'Right, clever man,' she says. 'So tell me, where is home?'

'If south is that way then home is in that direction.' I point to the wall.

She shrugs off her leather jacket and hangs it over the desk chair. 'And would I be able to see the room with the lights on?'

I turn the light on and take off my coat.

'It's nice,' she says.

'Yes.' I walk over to the bed, sit down and pull off my boots.

'Did you pick jasmine because I was coming?'

'Yes.'

She starts unbuttoning her shirt, then she stops. For a moment I can't read her expression, then I realise she is scared. I get up, lift her hair to one side and draw the shirt over her shoulders. It falls to the floor.

'Come,' I say. 'What happened the other night won't happen again.'

She kicks off her boots sitting on the side of the bed. 'I heard this program on the radio the other day,' she says. 'A professor,' she turns to me, 'said that human beings don't actually have a sense of direction.'

'Really?' I say. 'Does that mean that you and I are

equally good at finding our way?'

'Yep,' she laughs a little. And then she shrugs out of her jeans and her briefs.

I get undressed and pull the blanket over us. She reaches over and touches me. I put my arm around her waist and feel the bottom of her spine.

'Cats and dogs,' she continues and nudges closer, 'they have a sense of direction. Pigeons do as well. Scientists know exactly where in the brain that sense would be if we had it.'

Her voice is warm and fluid; it fills the room.

'You are so beautiful.' The words catch in my throat.

'Touch me,' she says.

'I won't last long.'

She adjusts herself on her back and watches my hand find its way.

'Remember,' she says, and sighs, 'remember the man on the wire? Philippe Petit. How he walked the tightrope in New York, from one tower to the other. Those beautiful towers.' She moans and guides my hand.

'Vera,' I say, thinking that I must have her, that I can't wait any longer, that my body will break if I don't.

'Wait,' she takes off her rings, leans over and puts them on the bedside table. Then she stiffens against me.

'What?' I say, as she pulls away from me.

'I can't believe this,' she says and stumbles out of bed.

'Have you gone completely mad?' There are goose bumps on her skin.

I scramble to sit up. 'What's happening?'

She starts pulling on her jeans.

'Vera? What's happening?'

'How could you?'

'What are you talking about?' But then I see it, the open notebook on the bedside table.

I get out of bed and touch her shoulder. 'Vera.'

She moves out of my reach and pulls on her shirt in jerky movements.

'It's nothing,' I say.

She crosses the floor and gets her jacket. 'My son is dead,' she says. 'My son is dead, but you're still looking for him. What's wrong with you?'

'He's my son too.' I turn around and reach for my pants, humiliated by my erection.

'Was,' says Vera. 'Ben *was*—he *is* no longer, David.' She puts her jacket on.

'Please,' I say. 'I wasn't looking for him on purpose. I was there to see Neil.'

She picks up her bag and walks to the door.

'Vera, please. Please don't go.'

She takes pity on me. I can see in her eyes that she is willing herself to stay. I can't bear the thought of her leaving.

She puts the bag down. And then she slowly walks

over and sits on the bed next to me.

'Vera,' I say. 'Could we just...'

'I don't want to talk,' she says.

'All right,' I say. 'What do you want to do?'

She lies down, facing away from me.

'Vera?' I say.

'I mean it, David. You have to stop talking.' She sounds drowsy, as if sleep has invaded her in a matter of seconds.

I sit there for a while longer and then she falls asleep. Her breathing is deep and steady and I wonder how she can possibly sleep after what has just happened between us.

I masturbate in the bathroom, carefully avoiding thinking about her. It's painful when I come. I get into the shower and stay there until my skin hurts too. Then I get dressed in sweatshirt and pants. If she's dressed then I will be too.

Before I get into bed I put the notebook in my bag.

I dream about my mother's pigeons. I dream about the way they lift in restless sprawling patterns, wings unfurling like the hands of flamenco dancers. In my dream my mother says, 'Pigeons always find their way home. They always come back.'

I wake early in the morning. The room is cold. Vera is asleep with her back to me, still in her leather jacket. I look at her shoulder rising and falling, knowing that I have probably destroyed everything.

Outside skies drift, grey against grey. I remember the dream and then I remember that my mother has come home. And I think of the many times she has come back from an overseas trip laden with presents, all of them somehow a testimony to her brilliance rather than gestures of love.

When Ben was five we spent a Christmas with her. Everything was perfect, of course. Goose, roasted potatoes, pudding, tissue-paper crowns and the biggest bonbons I have ever seen. Just back from Paris my mother gave Vera a book on a French photographer. Neil got a framed antique map of Mondovi in Algeria where Camus was born. Ben received a book on algebra puzzles that he really liked and I got a documentary of my hero, Sam Maloof, master furniture maker. And the presents kept coming.

But it felt like a show, just the way it always had when we were children. The conversation around the table was stifled. My mother told stories from her trip. Neil got drunk and Vera disappeared into the backyard with Ben after my mother suggested that we should reconsider our choice of gifts to him in the future. We had given him an Etch A Sketch and a marvellous red fire truck that was an instant hit.

'He has a great mind,' my mother said. 'He needs to be stimulated.'

'He's a child,' Vera said firmly. 'Not a project.'

Ben followed the conversation from his chair. 'What?' he said and looked up at Vera.

'Nothing, darling,' she said. 'Your grandma just likes to do things her way.'

I later found Vera lying on a blanket in the yard soaking up the sun. She was still wearing her green paper-tissue crown and her white dress was pulled up, showing off her tanned legs. Ben was playing with his fire truck next to her.

On the way home in the car Vera shook her head. 'It's a miracle you're not more damaged,' she said.

I grinned.

She laughed. 'You know what I mean.'

Ben was quiet in the back, drawing on the Etch A Sketch.

And then, with no houses in sight, we came across a road stall. We all got out of the car, Ben's hair blown here and there by the hot breeze. Three trays of strawberries, ripe and deep in colour, sat on a box covered with a red-and-white checked tablecloth. '$3 please' was written in crooked letters on a folded piece of cardboard taped to the cloth.

'Is it even strawberry season?' said Vera.

'Grandma wouldn't like that,' said Ben.

'Why?' I asked.

Ben thought for a while, then said, 'She didn't make

the stall.'

I started laughing. I couldn't stop.

Vera smiled and took my hand. 'They are beautiful,' she said to Ben. 'Why don't you see if we've got some coins in the glove compartment?'

We had enough for all three trays and devoured the juicy strawberries in the car with the air conditioning blasting.

'Wait,' said Vera as we were about to drive off.

She ran out and put a rock on the tablecloth.

'So it doesn't fly away,' she said, getting back in.

I sit up slowly. Vera is still asleep. The whole place feels sad somehow. The jasmine droops in the vase on the table and I can hear the shower tap dripping in the bathroom.

'Vera.' I reach over and touch her arm.

She turns onto her back and opens her eyes. And for a moment, before she remembers, she looks at me the way she used to.

Then she sits up. 'What time is it?'

'Just after seven,' I say. 'You wanted to get home early.'

She gets out of bed and walks to the window. Light falls on her cheek; she looks tired. 'A church?' she says with her back to me.

'The back of a church,' I say. 'Is the priest there?'

'No, there's no one.' She returns to the bed and collects

her rings from the bedside table.

I know she notices the absence of the notebook, but she doesn't say anything.

'I'll follow you to the train,' I say and push aside the doona. And for reasons I don't even try to comprehend I am compelled to put on my suit.

King Street is windy. A shop sign has been blown over by the wind. I stop to pick it up. Vera waits next to me, studying the window of a shop that sells second-hand clothes. One of the mannequins is missing an arm.

'Have coffee with me before you go,' I say. 'Please.'

She looks at her watch. 'I was hoping to catch the train in half an hour.'

'Take the one in an hour. Have a quick coffee and something to eat.'

She hesitates.

'Please,' I say.

'Okay.' She looks at me. 'Is there somewhere close?'

'There's a cafe around the corner.'

A plastic bag drifts past us and continues down the footpath. And I wonder for a moment, absurdly, if it's the same bag I saw two nights ago in Leichhardt. A fire truck speeds past and starts its siren right next to us. We both jump.

Vera stops. 'David, I really should go home. I forgot

to feed Ginger.'

'Ginger,' I say, 'has probably invited the whole cat neighbourhood over for a party. You'll spoil it if you come home early.'

It isn't funny and she doesn't smile.

The wind pulls at my jacket. I shiver and wonder why on earth I put on my suit. I reach over and take her hand even though she draws back from me. 'It's right there,' I point.

She hesitates.

'Just a quick coffee,' I say.

We're the only people outside; everyone else is huddled inside the warm cafe. Vera gets a woollen jumper from her bag and puts it on. Pigeons line the balustrade of the courthouse across from us. Three men in cheap suits hover together outside the entrance. I can't work out whether they are lawyers or awaiting trial.

A young woman with short brown hair brings our coffees, then returns with the croissant we ordered.

'They start early,' I say and nod to the men.

'Someone's always doing something wrong,' she says, then gestures to the croissant. 'Are you sharing?'

'Yes,' I nod.

'I'll get you an extra plate.'

The waitress returns with the plate and Vera watches

as I cut the croissant in half.

I want to tell Vera that it was a ghost I saw yesterday. I want to tell her that I'm over it, but I can't. Instead I say, 'I had a cake the other day. A lemon cake. It had flowers on it. I think they were pansies.'

It sounds ridiculous. I don't know what kind of flowers they were. I can't tell a tulip from a dahlia, and Vera knows it. But she nods as if I have just said something terribly interesting and continues to eat her share of the croissant.

I don't know what else to say. I suddenly can't take it. This is Vera, my wife, and we're sitting here like strangers.

'Vera,' I begin.

'Don't.'

I reach over and put a hand on her leg.

She pulls away, then says, 'My uncle was in jail for two years when I was little.'

I startle at this. 'Bunny?' I ask, seeing in my mind the kind-faced, chubby man that I have met a couple of times at family gatherings.

'He's the only uncle I have.' She leans forwards, puts her empty cup on the table and brushes the crumbs off her pants. 'I didn't see him for two years.'

'What did he do?'

'He ran over someone. Didn't stop. Only turned himself in a couple of days later. It was an accident, but he was a coward.'

'Why haven't you told me this?'

'What good would that have done?' She gets her bag and stands up.

'But why are you telling me now?'

'I don't know,' she says.

On our way to the station we cut across Victoria Park. There's a rally on. People are spilling out onto George Street and there is shouting and drumming and the smell of charred sausages hanging in the air. Two men are in the process of packing down a booth, and one of them stops to hand me pamphlets for Lifeline Australia and the Wilderness Society.

On the outskirts of the park we see a young girl walking on a tightrope strung between two tall fig trees. She wouldn't be much older than Ben. Her light brown hair is tied with a green elastic and her face is free of makeup. Her gaze is soft as she walks with her arms spread. There is such grace to the way she moves, it's almost like a dance. And I think of Vera last night, of her naked body and what she said about Philippe Petit and his tightrope walk. I remember the film clearly. I remember the look in his eyes when he walked out onto the rope and realised that he could do it. It was a triumphant look. When later he was asked why he had done it he answered, 'There is no why.' Vera and I had talked about that answer for days.

Vera observes the girl too, but doesn't say anything.

We continue down George Street in the wake of the rally. Things are left behind—stickers, balloons, Hungry Jack's food wrappers, and a sign saying 'No funding cuts for mental health programs' in green letters. The police are getting back on their motorcycles and barricades are being removed. And Vera keeps walking ahead of me. It's as if I'm not there at all.

I buy a ticket so I can walk onto the platform with Vera. Someone has spilled strawberry milk on the ground. The loudspeaker announces the departure.

'What do we do now?' I ask.

'I don't know,' she says.

Then she boards the train. The door closes and I watch her find a seat. She doesn't look back at me as the train leaves the platform.

The pressure on my chest is back; a solid, hard-cornered weight that pushes against my lungs. And I only just make it outside the station before I have to sit down on a bench. I force myself to breathe slowly. In and out. In and out.

A dirty-white terrier in a red collar appears next to me. It sniffs the hem of my trousers, then takes off. I turn to see who it belongs to, but neither the dog nor its owner is anywhere to be seen.

I am finding it hard to breathe; with every breath the pressure seems to increase. Cold sweat forms on my forehead and I can't help thinking that maybe I'm going mad. Maybe I'm seeing things that don't exist.

I pull out my phone and the Lifeline Australia pamphlet handed to me in the park and—like a drowning man reaching for a life buoy—I punch the number.

The phone rings twice, then a man answers and introduces himself as Con.

I already regret ringing, but the pressure on my chest is not going away. I tell Con my name.

A man hurries past me, phone pressed to his ear. A woman walks two feet behind him, dragging a large suitcase. I can't figure out whether they are together or not.

'And why are you calling today, David?'

The line is rehearsed, but he says my name with just the right amount of empathy. And it works. I can't help asking the question that is constantly on my mind.

'Why would someone run away from home?' I say.

'Run away?' he repeats.

'Yes, why would someone who is loved and cared for leave without a trace?'

'A young person?'

'He is twenty-four.'

'Your son?' asks Con.

'Yes.'

'The most common reason is mental illness.' Con speaks slowly as if he is considering every word he is saying. He continues, 'But of course there is the possibility that a crime has been committed.'

'I don't think there was any mental illness involved,' I say and feel an odd relief wash over me. Not from thinking that something terrible might have happened to Ben, but from talking to someone who is willing to think through the options with me.

'How long has your son been gone for?' says Con.

'Five months.'

'I presume the police are looking for him?'

The pressure in my chest eases a bit. 'They told us that people go missing all the time. Most return sooner or later.' Then I add, 'I thought I saw him yesterday.'

'You saw him?'

'I am almost certain it was him.'

'So you are searching for him?'

'No,' I say. 'It was a coincidence.'

'David,' he says, again with the empathetic voice, 'can I ask if you are married?'

I hesitate. 'Yes.'

'And your wife, how does she take it?'

The white dog is back. And now I see the owner: an overweight woman, sitting on a bench further down. She calls for the dog. I can't hear whether it's Sam or Stan, but either way the dog has decided to stay with me. It leans against my leg and views the pitiful entrance area with the stance of a king.

I am not mad after all.

'David?' Con prompts on the other end of the line. 'We don't have to talk about your wife. You are in control of this conversation; we can talk about anything you want.'

I hang up and don't even feel bad about it. I bend down to pat the dog. The pressure in my chest is almost gone. I wait a few more minutes, then I get up and head back to Newtown.

The processes of woodwork are predictable and calming, and I'm glad to lose myself in the work. I start by joining the sides of the chest. I secure the joints by putting a small piece of timber on top of them before hammering them into place. That protects the wood from being bruised. After that I begin the process of sanding. I work for several hours and it's only when I stop to get a drink of water that I check my phone. Vera would be home by now, but there are no messages from her. Instead I have two voicemails. The first is from Neil.

'David,' he says, 'I just spoke to Vera. She wouldn't tell me what happened last night, but she's upset. Are you okay? Call me back. Please, mate, just call.' He hangs up.

I don't call back.

The second message is from Shaggy, my old uni friend. We see each other about once a year, still bound together by the fact that we left uni not only on the same day, but at the same time. We marched out in the middle of a sociology lecture and proceeded to get insanely drunk while sitting on Shaggy's surfboard in the college dorm. Later he escaped to Coogee Beach and I moved down the road to the butcher's workshop.

I ring him back.

He picks up. 'Benny Bobcat.' Neither of us can remember how that nickname came about and I'm thankful that he's the only one who remembers it. 'Mate,' he continues, 'I just wanted to see how you're going. We haven't talked for ages.'

Not since the funeral, I think. Not since the funeral when he had worn an ill-fitted suit and combed his long bleached hair so vigorously that it sat oddly to one side. For weeks afterwards it was Shaggy's effort to comb his hair that stayed with me more than anything else said and done that day.

'I'm in Sydney,' I say. 'Are you around today? I could catch the bus over in an hour or two.'

'Of course,' he says. 'Give me a call when you're close. I'll be at the beach.'

—

The ocean outside the bus window is flat and there is hardly anyone around. A red and yellow lifesaver flag billows in the wind. A buggy is parked nearby and the air smells of seaweed.

Once Vera and I met up with Shaggy here. It was summer and two weeks before she gave birth to Ben. There were people everywhere, overflowing garbage bins, thongs and scorched skin. The smell of coconut oil hung thick in the air. I held her hand and tried to stop people from bumping into her.

Vera hadn't liked Coogee very much. It was right after Keating's Redfern address and we were both inspired. 'Things are changing out there,' Vera said, as we walked towards the beach, 'but no one here seems to care about anything but getting a tan.'

She looked like a defiant warrior princess despite the polka-dot swimsuit she was wearing. The swimsuit was so unlike her—almost like the dress she had worn the first night we met—and I don't recall ever seeing it again.

The ocean was huge that day. Waves rolled in, one after the other, regular and precise as clockwork. Vera and I swam out past the break and bobbed in the ocean next to each other, rising and falling with each surge. We stayed there for ages. The voices of the beach faded and it was just Vera and me, and the deep pull of the sea.

At one stage Vera had looked over at me. She had tears

in her eyes. 'It's almost too beautiful,' she said.

I get off the bus and find Shaggy on the beach. He is sitting near the lifesavers' office gazing at the ocean, wearing a worn Billabong wetsuit.

'Man,' he says as I sit down next to him. He pats me awkwardly on the back and passes me a beer in a brown paper bag. 'I come prepared,' he says.

'Have you been out today?' I nod towards the ocean.

'Naw,' he says. 'But they're promising a change this afternoon.'

'Where's your board?'

He points at the purple longboard leaning against the wall behind us.

'New?' I ask

'Yeah.'

'Looks good.'

We sit like that for a couple of hours. We don't talk much. At dusk the ocean starts to swell and Shaggy becomes restless.

I get up to leave. Shaggy gives me a sideways hug, and on impulse I say, 'I think Ben is still alive.'

'Yeah,' he says and nods. 'There are stranger things between heaven and earth.' He looks out philosophically towards the sea. 'A good kid, that Ben.'

I stop on the boardwalk to see him catch the first

wave, then I walk to the main street and take the first bus back to Newtown.

The bus snakes its way through the industrial neighbourhood of Alexandria, past closed factory outlets, dingy back lanes and lock-up garages. Along Mitchell Road garbage bins are lined up like soldiers. It's almost dark by the time we pass Sydney Park. The four chimneys stand out against the evening sky.

Turning into King Street I spot a cafe that's open and get off the bus to buy something for dinner.

'They're big,' says the young man behind the counter, as he clumsily wraps the sandwich. He has a crew cut and wears a nose ring.

A homeless man with matted hair and a long beard passes the shop, pulling a rattling shopping trolley behind him.

The young man hands me the sandwich and nods towards the homeless man. 'They sleep in the park,' he says. 'Near the chimneys. I spent a night there once. My dad threw me out, in the middle of winter.'

'That must have been cold,' I say.

'I couldn't feel my feet in the morning.'

My phone rings as I leave the shop—it's Maria. I answer while watching the homeless man walk to the park. Cars are buzzing past. Lights flicker and fall.

'David,' she says. 'I've been trying to reach you.'

'Maria,' I say. 'I really don't want to talk about it.'

She is quiet for a second, then says, 'Talk about what?'

'About Vera and me.'

A bus roars past.

'Where are you? It sounds noisy,' she says.

'On King Street.'

'Can you hear me?'

'Hold on a moment,' I say and cross the road. And without thinking I follow the homeless man into the park. Three runners in black spandex and neon-coloured shoes pass me, chatting breathlessly.

The chimneys sit on my right. A path of dotted lights leads deeper into the park. It's like entering a mystical landscape of hills and lakes.

'Sorry, are you still there?' I start to climb the hill nearest to me.

'Yes,' she says. 'David, I need to speak to you, but I don't think we should do it on the phone.'

I reach the top and see the airport beyond the park. 'Maria, I don't want to discuss my marriage. Really. Neil keeps ringing too.'

'That's not why I'm calling,' she says. 'Could we meet tomorrow morning? I could come to Newtown.'

Maria has never asked to meet me before. I sit down on the cold grass and say, 'Is everything okay?'

'No,' she says. 'No, it's not. But I'll see you tomorrow morning. We can talk then.' Then she hangs up.

If it's not about Vera and me then it can only be about Neil and his drinking.

An intervention. That's the last thing I need.

A bird calls out in the direction of the lake, but otherwise everything is quiet. In the distance a plane ascends into the night sky.

The first word Ben said was 'Fly' or more like 'Fi'. He would say, 'Fi, fi, fi,' when we swooped his plush aeroplane over him. He had two teeth and the sweetest smile. And he continued to love planes. When he was five I took him to Sydney. It was autumn. The weather was still warm and the sky clear. We drove to a park at Botany Bay near the airport. Ben bounced ahead as I opened the boot. He ran across the grass towards a small group of plane spotters and joined a man in his fifties with drooping cheeks.

I unloaded the boot and tried to persuade Ben to come and sit on the blanket with me, but by then the man was already demonstrating the wondrous workings of his radio scanner.

'Ben's fine,' the man said. 'He can stay with me if he wants.'

As I spread out the picnic blanket nearby I marvelled over the fact that Ben had already introduced himself. I drank the tea Vera had made and watched them chat until it was time to go.

'Ben's a special kid,' said the man when we said good-bye. 'He can talk to anyone. It's a gift.'

A lonesome runner passes the foot of the hill. He continues towards the chimneys and I notice a bonfire along the brick wall. The light illuminates the tarpaulin that covers some of the holes in the brickwork. It looks like a make-shift camp site.

Then it strikes me. What if Ben has decided to live here? I stand up and fuelled by the possibility I walk down the hill. Ben has never been shy or judgemental. Everything and everyone interests him.

The air is different near the chimney. The crisp smell of grass is gone. Instead it smells of unwashed bodies, rancid milk and petrol from the bonfire. Empty bottles and chocolate wrappers litter the ground.

I pass the holes in the wall. Every single one seems occupied. Some are empty, but filled with belongings: pillows, blankets, shoes and plastic bags. Others are covered over with tarps.

The homeless man with the rattling trolley sits next to the fire. He's younger than I first thought, perhaps even younger than me.

'I'm sorry to disturb you,' I say.

His beard is matted and he smells so bad that I have to breathe through my mouth, but his eyes are kind and present.

'Looking for someone?' His voice is strangely melodic.

'Yes.'

'Everyone is looking for someone,' he says. 'Who?'

'A young man, his name is Ben.'

'Your son?'

'Yes,' I nod.

'Only one young fellow around,' says the man and I notice spittle in his beard. 'The last hole, the one with the blue tarp. He has a dog. Don't touch it, it bites.'

'Thank you,' I say, then remember the food I am carrying. 'Would you like a sandwich?' I lift the brown paper bag for him to see.

'Most obliged,' says the man.

The possibility that Ben might be just a few steps ahead makes me feel short of breath. I want to stretch out the moment as long as possible before I check. I search my mind for something to talk about, but the man has already turned away from me and is moaning quietly.

'Are you okay?' I ask.

He stares back at me as if he has never seen me before. I wait, but when he doesn't answer I walk to the end of the brick wall.

A pair of dirty bare feet sticks out from under the blue

tarp. They could be Ben's. My heart pounds as I pull the tarp to the side.

The boy bolts upright and the dog growls.

'What the fuck do you want?' His hair is blond and his fists clenched. He looks like a small child coming out of a deep sleep.

'I'm sorry,' I say. 'I'm looking for my son, Ben. He's twenty-three. No, twenty-four.'

'You don't know how old your own fucking son is?' He reaches for a backpack pushed up against the wall.

'He's twenty-four,' I say.

'And what did you do, old man? Slap him around? Punch him up?' He pulls out a packet of cigarettes.

'No,' I say. 'Of course not.'

The hole stinks. A sour stench of bad breath and shit.

He lights the cigarette and inhales deeply. 'You're all the same,' he says and spits on the ground. 'Liars, all of you.'

'That's not true.'

'Well, he's gone missing for some fucking reason, hasn't he?' The boy laughs, baring teeth brown and rotten.

When I get back to the house I sit at the desk and look out into the night. I know that I'm missing something. The boy in the park was right. There must be a reason why Ben disappeared. There must be some kind of explanation, but no matter how hard I try I can't seem to figure it out.

I spot the priest across the lane. He sits on the back stairs again. The light from the open door illuminates his red hair as he blows smoke rings into the night.

I want to run downstairs and insist that he listen. I want to give him a list of all the things that have happened from Ben's birth right up until now. I want to give it all to him for him to examine. But at the same time I can't bear to think that this man, this priest, might be able to pinpoint exactly what it was that made Ben leave. Because what if it's to do with me? How do I live with that?

I smell coffee as I am getting dressed the next morning. Pat must be downstairs. I check my phone standing by the window and realise that it's raining again. There are two missed calls from Neil. Fat drops streak the window and outside everything is grey. I force myself not to think about the lack of contact from Vera as I walk downstairs.

Pat is wearing a bright red T-shirt under an oversized woollen cardigan.

'You look like you're ready to work,' she says.

'This is how I always look,' I say and attempt a smile. 'Although yesterday I wore a suit and almost ended up in a rally.'

'Do you want coffee?'

'Yes, please.' I sit down at the table. 'Are you going to

have some?'

'I've already had two. I was here early.' She puts a cup in front of me and sits down. 'I don't go to demonstrations and I always feel bad about it.'

I taste the coffee. It's strong and good.

'Anyway,' she continues, 'I'm sure you wouldn't have stood out wearing a suit. I know plenty of people who work in offices and go to rallies on their lunch break.'

'I went to an anti-war protest once in a suit,' I say. And I remember Ben in his stroller, perfectly content amid all the noise and the people. 'It was twenty years ago. I'd come straight from a meeting and didn't have time to change. I was punched in the face by a guy twice my size.'

I recall lying on the ground and seeing Vera jump on the man's back like a crazy person to stop him from punching me again.

'And what happened?' asks Pat.

'He ended up apologising. He said that I looked "aloof", that I reminded him of his dad.'

'And are you?' asks Pat.

'What?'

'Aloof?'

'No,' I say, surprised by her seriousness. 'Why would you think that?'

'You just seem...a bit reserved, somehow.'

I'm stunned and just about to ask her why, when

someone knocks on the door.

The smell of wet leaves fills the room as Pat lets Maria in.

'You're early.' I get up to greet her.

'I know,' she says, and leans her umbrella against the wall. 'Do you mind?' She looks from Pat to me. 'I can come back if you're in the middle of something.'

'No, it's fine,' I say. 'We can go upstairs.'

'Stay here,' says Pat, 'I'm all done.' She gets her raincoat and gives us a quick wave as she leaves.

'There's more coffee if you want some.' I give Maria a hug.

'Yes, please.' She takes off her scarf and sits down.

I walk to the kitchenette. Leaden light falls through the windows and touches the wooden floorboards.

'Is Pat a friend?' Maria asks as I hand her the cup.

'No,' I say. 'She runs this place.'

'You seem friendly.'

'She's nice,' I say and sit down.

Maria reaches for the sugar bowl. There is a Mickey Mouse bandaid on her index finger.

'What happened to your hand?' I remember how Ben loved his Winnie the Pooh bandaids. Once he wore one on every finger for a whole week. Vera had to pry them off him in fear that he was going to get a fungus.

'I chopped tomatoes last night and forgot what I was

[143]

doing.' Maria stirs the coffee.

Again I am struck by the change in her, but I can't put a finger on what it is. She still looks tired, but is perfectly done up as always—her lips painted, her dark hair in an immaculate ponytail.

A car accelerates past on the laneway outside.

Maria puts the spoon down. 'I'm sorry. I know this is the last thing you need, but I really do need to talk with you.'

'I'm not sure I can do this,' I say.

'It's just…I have no one else,' she says.

I look down at the table. Someone has scratched the initials 'S. N.' into the thin lacquer.

'Something happened that day,' she continues.

I look up at her, confused.

'I left the door open,' she says. 'I didn't imagine that anyone would just walk in.'

It takes me a moment to realise that she's talking about the break-in.

'I was letting air through the house,' she continues. 'I had just washed the floors and went to make tea. He was standing in the middle of the living room when I came back. There were dirty footprints all over the wet floor.'

Red patches appear on her cheeks.

'There was something wrong with his eyes. I knew it right away. Something horribly wrong. He came right up close and I asked, "What do you want?" But he didn't answer, he didn't say anything at all, he just put a hand around my throat and squeezed.'

'He tried to strangle you?'

'If it hadn't been for Jared I would have been dead. He came running in from the garden and started yelling and shouting and the man let me go, just like that. And then he left.'

'I'm so sorry,' I say. 'I didn't know.'

'I'm scared all the time, David. I can't sleep, I can't eat. The other day I had a panic attack at the shopping mall. They had to call an ambulance. I thought I was going to die.'

'Is someone helping you through this?'

'I'm going to leave Neil.'

'What?' I say.

'I have to.'

'But you love Neil,' I say.

Maria takes off the scarf and I can see faint grey bruises on her neck. 'I always thought,' she says, 'that if I was a good wife and a good mother then I would get some kind of return. Like a safe passage for me and the people I love.' She tries to laugh, but it sounds more like a sob. 'I thought that if I just did everything right then I would be able to control the future. But then this man walks into my house and destroys everything.'

'What if I could talk Neil into moving house?' I ask.

She shakes her head. 'There's something I'm not getting, something I need to find. I just don't know what it is. I need to start over, David. To go back to the beginning.'

'But what about counselling?' I say. 'It could help you figure all that out. It could help Neil too. We both know he drinks too much.'

The sound of the rain increases. There is a low rumble of thunder in the distance.

'No,' she stands up. 'I just came to make sure that you'll be there for Neil.'

'Maria, please don't go. There must be something we can do. Think about Jared.'

'Jared will be fine. He's got two parents who love him.' She looks at me steadily. 'Please, will you promise me?'

'Of course I'll look after Neil,' I say.

She kisses me on the cheek. 'Don't tell him before I get a chance to speak to him. I'll do it soon.'

I walk upstairs feeling immensely sad for Maria and Neil. I sit down near the window and look out onto the rain. A woman with blonde hair and a red raincoat pauses in the lane to put up her umbrella.

I remember Neil the other night, swaying drunkenly to the Ramones. Sweet, pompous Neil. As much as he talks about his love for Marx, Maria has been the centre of his world for as long as they have known each other.

I get my phone and do the only thing I can think of doing for him right now. I dial my mother's number. As the phone rings I imagine her at her desk with the green lamp lit and papers spread out in front of her. Her intimate world. Her fortress, from which she lives and rules.

She picks up on the second ring. 'Beatrice Oliver speaking.' Her voice is as authoritative and charismatic as ever.

'Neil told me you'd come home,' I say.

'A few days ago.'

'How was Arizona?'

'It was hot,' she says. 'The faculty was brilliant, but the desert was even more brilliant. Cowboys and cactuses, you know. They offered me a position. I'm considering taking it.'

'And you're not going to ask me how we've been?'

'Are you going to be mad at me, darling? Because if you are then we might have to do this another time, I am terribly jetlagged.'

I take a deep breath. 'I'm in Sydney,' I say and watch the rain splatter on the windowpane. 'I was thinking of coming for a visit.'

'Neil hinted that you might be leaving Vera. I was hoping it wasn't true.'

A flock of galahs, radiantly pink, gather under a tree in the wet lane.

'I haven't left Vera,' I say.

I'm not angry with Neil. He still tells our mother almost everything. He has done it for as long as I can remember, hoping, I am sure, to be loved in return. Once when we were teenagers I caught him having a very adult cup of tea with my mother while earnestly discussing the details of a secret I had confided in him earlier.

The galahs scatter when a man walks past on the lane. He walks quickly, backpack lifted over his head as a shield against the rain. I see the Che Guevara patch on the backpack and recognise the lanky walk.

'Ten tomorrow,' I yell. I throw the phone on the desk and sprint down the stairs and out into the rain. By the time I reach the lane Ben has disappeared from view.

I run as fast as I can, trying not to slip on the wet leaves. My footsteps ring against the bitumen and within seconds I reach the end of the lane. I am soaked through, gasping for breath, and I can't see him anywhere. 'Ben,' I call out. 'Ben!' I turn left and start running again. A dog scampers out of my way and into a yard. Its fur stands up in wet tufts. A car races by, spraying water all over the footpath. I come to a halt when I see a woman in a black raincoat chaining her bike to a fence. She instinctively takes a step back when she sees me. 'Sorry,' I say. 'Have you seen a young man pass by?' She shakes her head. The bike lock in her hand is a fluorescent green.

I stop at the next intersection, panting. My chest burns and I can't see him anywhere. I start walking in the direction of his flat. Ahead the city is erased by fog and rain.

Ben's apartment is empty. Everything is where I left it: the gnome is on the table, the pink shirt on the bed. The place reeks of alcohol and I open the door to the rain-drenched balcony. Music drifts in from the flat next door.

I put the kettle on while drying my hair with a towel and then I find a packet of tea. The music next door changes from some unidentifiable rock to a piece that I recognise. It's a piano piece by Philip Glass, one that Ben likes.

I walk across the landing and knock on the door. A woman opens. It's the same woman I met the other night. She is dressed in sweatshirt and jeans. Her hair is up and there's something wholesome about her, something reminiscent of farm life and full-cream milk.

'Hi,' I say, aware that I am drenched and look a mess. 'I'm Ben's dad. Ben from next door.'

'I was wondering when you would come,' she says.

'When I would come?' I repeat, but she doesn't seem to hear me.

'I don't have long, but come in for a moment,' she says and steps aside for me to enter.

Her flat is the mirror image of Ben's, but it feels lighter. The curtains are white and her bedspread is bright blue. A cup of tea sits on the table.

She turns the music off. Cold air comes through the open balcony door and I shiver in my wet clothes. And then I notice the garden gnome that sits, shiny with rain, in a cluster of succulents. It matches the one I found on Ben's balcony.

She reaches over and shakes my hand. 'I'm Alice,' she says. 'But you already know that.'

'No,' I say. 'I'm sorry, but I have no idea who you are.'

She looks at me, surprised. 'I thought Neil would have told you. Or your mum?'

I'm taken aback. 'You and Ben were together?'

She gets her bag from the dresser. 'Neil said you took Ben's death hard.' She looks at me. 'Maybe that's why he didn't tell you. Sorry, I just need to pack a few things while we're talking. I'm starting a new job today, so I can't be late.'

'How long were you together?'

She pulls out a white shirt from a drawer. 'Since our trip to India,' she says and adds the shirt to the bag. 'We both went with Engineers Without Borders. And later, when this flat became available, I moved in.' She picks up an umbrella and places it next to the bag. 'It was almost like living together, you know. It made it really difficult when we broke up.'

'And when was that?' I ask, thinking that maybe it's all her fault. Maybe this innocent-looking farm girl is to blame for all that's happened.

She stops what she's doing and looks at me. 'Ben left me two months before he went missing. I didn't even know he was gone. I had already stopped knocking on his door, stopped ringing him. And I spent most of that time at home with my mum anyway. I didn't know what'd happened before Neil came around one day and told me.' She closes her bag. 'I'm really sorry, but I have to go.'

'Why did he leave you?'

She shrugs. 'He didn't give me a reason, he just said that there were things he needed to do.'

'Was he behaving differently in any way?'

'He was his usual self.'

'And what was that?'

'Restless,' she says. 'Always pushing boundaries.' She takes her cup to the sink.

'What did he like doing?'

'Walking across the Sydney Harbour Bridge in the middle of the night, running out of restaurants without paying, or getting locked into the state library after closing hours. He was impulsive and totally crazy, and I loved him. But all that stuff was rarely fun for me.' She looks at me. 'Except for the night he turned up unexpectedly in a borrowed a car. We drove down the coast to Neil's house, bought some bread and cheese on the way, and stayed there for a whole week, just him and me.' She tears up.

I wait.

'He used to say he wanted a relationship like the one you and your wife have, and I thought...I know we were young, but I thought it might be us, you know?'

'Did he ever talk about taking his own life?'

She shook her head. 'Never. I would have done something about it straight away. My aunty works for Lifeline. But, look, I'm sorry, I really do have to go. Maybe you could come back later?'

'Just one last thing,' I say. 'Did anything else happen around the time he broke up with you?'

She hesitates. 'He started hanging out with this guy he was working with at Wanders.'

'Wanders?'

'A cafe down on King Street. It's pretty grungy. That's where he met Kaiser.'

'I didn't know he had a job,' I say.

'You weren't close.'

'We used to be,' I say and feel the pressure on my chest again. 'We used to be really close.'

She puts the bag over her shoulder. 'I need to go,' she says.

'Sorry,' I say. And then I get my wallet out and hand

her one of my business cards. 'I want you to have my number and I want you to ring me if you see him.'

She looks at me. For a moment everything is dead quiet, then she blushes and her eyes flood.

'I want you to go,' she says.

I'm about to tell her that I'm not crazy, but she backs away from me and reaches for her phone.

'You need to leave right now,' she says, 'or I'll call the police.'

By the time I make it back to the house it has stopped raining and a feeble rainbow paints the sky. My pants cling to my legs and my feet are numb with cold. I get out of my clothes in the bathroom, but I am too angry to shower. Instead I march naked into the living room and dial Neil's number.

'Finally, David,' he says, answering the phone. 'I've left you about ten messages.'

I don't bother saying hello. 'You didn't tell me Ben had a girlfriend,' I say.

There is a pause, then Neil clears his throat and says, 'Listen, mate—'

'Why would you keep something like that from me? What's going on, Neil?'

'Nothing is going on. It just wasn't up to me to break the news. If it makes you feel any better I asked Ben to tell you.'

'How the fuck is that going to make me feel better?' I ask.

'What's got into you, mate?'

'How exactly is it going to make me feel better that you and Ben are best pals?'

'We *were* best pals,' he corrects me. 'All I was trying to do was to be a good uncle.'

'You took him away from me,' I say and it feels good to get it out. It should have been said a long time ago.

'What are you talking about?'

'Always getting together, always lending him books. You even lent them your fucking beach house, Neil. How could you not tell us about Alice?'

He clears his throat. 'I did tell Vera.'

'What?'

'After Ben died I told her. She was happy that he had been seeing someone.'

'She didn't tell me.' I sit down on the bed; my skin is grey in the overcast light.

'That's not on me, mate.'

'Can you stop calling me "mate" for just one fucking moment, you fuckwit? I'm your brother. You should have told me, not her.'

When Neil speaks again he uses that low warm voice of his, the one he no doubt uses on his most troublesome students. 'Vera was afraid you would try and talk to Alice.

And, to be honest, so was I. Alice doesn't need that.' He says her name as if they are close friends and I want to punch him.

I hear him light a cigarette and inhale. 'Are you in Newtown?'

'Yes.'

'Meet me at the Vietnamese place on King Street. I need some lunch. This marking is doing my head in.'

'What end of King Street?' I ask, already pulling jeans and a sweatshirt out of the drawers. This conversation is far from over.

The restaurant is called Saigon Palace and is near Sydney Park. Plastic flowers hang from bamboo racks in the ceiling and flute music plays on the stereo. An elderly woman with heavy eye makeup sits on a stool behind the counter. She takes her eyes off the TV to hand me a menu as I walk in.

Neil sits at the back. Walking through the restaurant I pass a couple sharing a steaming hot pot.

'I ordered,' Neil says as I sit down.

The plates glisten with oil. There is pork belly, a beef stir fry, a curry and a plate of greens, and I wonder, not for the first time, how Neil manages to stay thin. He's on his second Carlsberg.

It's clear that Maria hasn't talked to him yet, but I am

so angry that I can't feel the slightest bit sorry for him. I stare at him and wait.

He puts the chopsticks down and wipes his mouth. 'David,' he says, 'what would you have done if I had told you about Alice?'

I shrug.

'Would you have gone straight to her place and asked her about Ben?' he continues.

'Someone should have asked her,' I say. 'We still don't know what happened.'

'I asked her, David, of course I did. But they broke up, mate. She didn't even know he'd gone missing.' Neil wipes his forehead with the paper napkin. 'This damn chilli gets me every time.'

'I think you should say sorry,' I say.

'What?' He puts the napkin down. His hair falls in his face.

'I think you should say sorry.'

'To you?'

'Yes.'

'David, don't be so childish.' He motions to the woman behind the bar. On the TV David Attenborough gently pats a bison, shielding his eyes from the sun.

'I want you to apologise,' I insist, more loudly this time.

The couple with the hotpot glance at us.

The woman brings another round of beers.

'Thank you.' Neil looks up at her.

She nods and walks back to her seat.

Neil picks up his beer, then looks at me. 'All right,' he says. 'I'm sorry, mate. I mean it. It was wrong to keep it from you.'

'You saw him all the time, Neil. Why didn't you see that something was wrong?'

'We didn't speak much towards the end.'

'Why?' I ask. 'What are you not telling me?' Then I remember Vera's last exhibition and how they were barely talking and it dawns on me. 'You had a fight?'

'It's fucking...we were such good mates.'

'What about? What were you fighting about, Neil?'

He shakes his head. 'It was stupid.'

'Neil, I'm warning you, I have no patience.' I stare at him.

He hesitates, then says, 'Ben wanted to stop his studies. I tried to talk him out of it.'

'Stop his studies?'

'I couldn't talk sense into him.'

'But why did he want to quit? I don't understand.'

'He wanted to go back to Rajasthan. He wanted to learn how to fly a plane.' Neil slams a fist on the table. 'I'm still so fucking angry with him.'

I look at him incredulously.

'He wanted to fly, David. He wanted to fly and I yelled at him.' Neil takes a swig of beer. 'There's a small airport near the desert in Rajasthan. You can get a licence for hardly any money. Ben went there when he was doing work for Engineers Without Borders.'

'I don't believe it.'

'It was impossible to talk sense into him,' says Neil. 'I tried. He called me "a fucking imperialist".'

I almost smile, thinking, *That's my boy*. That would have hurt Neil more than anything else Ben could have thrown at him.

'I loved him, David. I wasn't trying to take him away from you.'

'Why didn't you tell me he wanted to go to India?' I say. 'We could have gone; we could have looked for him.'

'Don't you think that we would have been on the first plane there if they hadn't found him right away?'

'You're keeping things from me.'

'That's all, mate. That's all I know.'

'You didn't tell me what happened to Maria,' I say.

'You spoke to her?'

'Why didn't you?'

He shrugs. 'There was nothing you could do.'

'That's not the point,' I say.

He looks at me earnestly. 'I'm your big brother, remember?'

'We're not children any more.'

'I'm still your big brother and you're going through something terrible. I didn't want to burden you.'

The couple across from us gets up to pay.

I look at the leftover food on our table. I have no appetite at all. And then I have a sudden memory of Neil and me, teenagers strutting down Norton Street eating gelato, full of life. Now I just feel sad for both of us.

I look at Neil. 'I rang mum,' I say. 'I'm seeing her tomorrow.'

He looks at me in surprise. 'That's bloody good, mate. Bloody great.' He reaches over and pats me on the arm. 'I appreciate it.' Then he leans back in the chair. 'Mate, it's hell without you. She is not easy.' He reaches inside his coat for a cigarette.

'I'm pretty sure you're not allowed to smoke in here,' I say.

He turns in his chair and raises the cigarette questioningly to the woman behind the counter. She gives him a thumbs up, then looks back at the TV.

'I come here all the time,' he says. 'It's okay when there's no one around. You should have the sticky rice dessert. It's good.'

'I'm fine,' I say.

'Damn rules,' he grumbles softly. 'The whole city is turning into a mausoleum. A damn monument to health.

But what happens to life, hey? Did anyone ask Sartre if it was healthy to smoke, or Camus?'

'Probably not,' I say.

His voice gets louder. 'Every damn picture of Camus is of him smoking and have you ever seen anyone cooler-looking than Camus?'

I think of Neil dancing to the Ramones, pipe in hand, his body tall and thin.

He stubs the cigarette on the plate. 'What are you doing with the rest of the day, brother?

'Working on a chest.'

He nods. 'It's a good little workshop.' He puts the packet of cigarettes in his shirt pocket. 'Look, mate. Could you let me know if Mum seems different to you? It's probably nothing. I mean, she has just started writing a new book, for fuck's sake, but I'd like to know what you think.'

That night I dream of Ben's hands at different stages: when he was five, eight and ten. And then again when he was eighteen and crying in my arms. In my dream I marvel over the fact that his hands have become those of a man. When I wake the memory of him pushes into the daylight, running ahead of me; a jolting electric shock that tumbles out of bed on unstable legs. How could he not be alive? How could he not be alive when I remember him so clearly?

My mother looks the same—tall and vibrant, with the same restless, captivating energy. She is wearing a dark green jumper and jeans and looks at me curiously, warmly even, as if nothing is wrong.

I follow her down the corridor to the kitchen, past what used to be our old rooms, long since remodelled to host visiting scholars.

The door to her room is open. A suitcase sits on the bed.

'I'm still unpacking,' she says. 'And freezing. I haven't adjusted to winter yet. Come into the kitchen, I have the heater on.'

The kitchen is one of the few places that doesn't hold books. The back wall has been opened up and the glass doors allow a view of the small concreted yard and the bird shed at the back. She renovated the space after Neil and I moved out, adding new cupboards and a stainless steel bench. In the centre of the kitchen sits the beech table that I made her early in my career, decent but not fantastic.

I unpack the cake that I bought on the way over. It's from the same place as the one Pat bought for us the other day.

My mother puts the kettle on and rinses the teapot in the sink. I can smell the smokiness of the dregs.

'I know that bakery,' she says and nods at the cake. 'It's a wonderful place, isn't it? So creative.' She flashes me

a brilliant smile, the kind of smile that knocks you sideways and makes you remember long-forgotten childhood
dreams; adventures in deep woods or drinking cocoa in a
space-shuttle light-years away from earth.

I put the cake on a plate and wonder how she manages
to pretend that nothing is wrong and why once again I'm
succumbing to her charm. I remember the time we all
went out to a Greek restaurant in the city. My mother had
turned to me at the table and asked what I thought of her
newest book and before I could stop myself I said, 'I think
you're amazing.'

'Amazing?' She tasted the word and I could see it
wasn't to her liking.

On the way home Vera had said, 'Why would you do
that? Why would you open yourself up to her like that?'

'I forgot,' I said.

'How could you forget? You spent an entire childhood
with her.'

I shook my head. 'I honestly don't know.'

'Did Neil tell you that the department lent me a yellow
Mustang while I was in Arizona?' My mother reaches for
the tea jar.

'I really don't want to hear about it,' I say.

'David, please don't be angry with me.'

'You left three days after the funeral. You just left.'

She walks over and opens the door to the backyard. Cold air rushes in. Two noisy miners swoop over the bird shed.

'They tease the pigeons relentlessly,' she says.

'That's it?' I say. 'You've got nothing to say?'

'Go and have a look at the birds, David,' she says, without looking at me. 'I'll bring the tea out in a moment.'

I don't move.

'Please,' she says.

The door to the shed is open. The smell of hay and bird droppings hangs in the air. There are twelve of them, all in individual cages. They are different in colour—brown, white, grey. Light falls on their beaks and eyes and I think, not for the first time, that my mother and her pigeons make up an unlikely love affair.

She crosses the yard and hands me a cup of tea, then eases a brown and white spotted bird out of its cage. 'This little one is Harriet,' she says. The bird nestles between her hands, heart beating visibly against her palm. 'I haven't had time to go down the coast this year. I think they're longing for a big flight.' Then she nods in the direction of the neighbour's garden. 'Edda was looking after them while I was gone, but of course I couldn't ask her to go down the coast.'

I look at the neighbouring garden with its orange tree

and long garden beds covered in nets. Edda is my mother's age and she was kind to Neil and me when we were growing up.

My mother gently caresses the pigeon's head before opening the cage door again, but the pigeon takes off unexpectedly and flutters into the grey sky. We follow its flight past trees and electrical wires and for a wild moment I want Harriet to continue over the rooftops and never ever come back.

My mother remains calm. 'I went to a carnival in the Arizona desert,' she says, keeping an eye on the pigeon. 'They had show planes, old ones, and they were spraying yellow and red all over that bright Arizona sky. It was magnificent.'

The pigeon swerves gracefully and dives. 'Here she comes,' says my mother and the pigeon lands on the ledge and walks straight into the cage.

'Watching those planes in the desert,' my mother closes the cage door, 'was my way of saying goodbye to Ben. He would have loved it. It was my funeral for him.' She looks at me. 'I needed to get away, David. His death took everything out of me.' Her voice breaks. 'I wasn't sure if I was going to get through the pain of it. Forgive me, you're angry with me, I understand. But just know it was all I could do.'

I don't know how to respond. I stare at the birds and

feel utterly alone.

'Let's go inside,' says my mother. 'It's freezing out here.'

She cuts the cake at the table. 'Did Neil tell you that I'm working on a new book?' The knife runs smoothly through the creamy icing. She places a piece of cake on my plate. 'I'm going right back to the beginning, to Freud. Did you know, by the way, that his couch was filled with horsehair?'

'No,' I say.

'When I was in Vienna last year I went to the Freud Museum. It was an extraordinary place, it was...' My mother stops talking and for a moment it looks as if she doesn't know where she is.

'What?' I ask.

She shakes her head. 'Nothing, darling. I'm just tired.'

'You knew,' I say.

'Knew what?'

'That Ben wanted to fly.'

'But of course I knew,' she says, then realises: 'You didn't?'

'He was two months away from finishing his degree.'

'Ben was extraordinary,' she says. 'He wanted to live an extraordinary life.'

'You encouraged him to go.'

'Yes, I did.'

'How could you?'

'How could I not? Ben was...he was the light of my life.' She reaches for a serviette. 'He was exceptional,' she says and blows her nose, 'but you couldn't see it, David, you just couldn't see it. You wanted him to be like you.'

I get up from the table and reach for my coat. 'I'll see myself out,' I say.

She grabs my arm. 'David, stay. I didn't mean...' She stops mid-sentence, then says, 'Are you going?'

I don't bother to answer.

'David.' She follows me down the hallway.

I walk out the front door without saying goodbye. My heart is pounding. I can't even stand looking at her.

Then she calls out, 'Bring Ben next time.'

I turn. 'What?'

She looks confused. 'I didn't say anything.'

I walk back towards her. 'You asked me to bring Ben next time.'

'Have you gone mad? Why would I do that?'

'Mum,' I say and touch her arm. 'You need to see a doctor.'

Before I know what's happening she lashes out and scratches my face, and I react without thinking. I slap her hard on the cheek, very hard, and she stumbles backwards and only doesn't fall because I reach out to grab her. She stares at me, the skin on her cheek a defiant pink.

'Mum,' I say.

'Go.' She wrestles out of my grip. 'You need to go.'

'I'm sorry.'

She turns away from me and walks down the hallway.

'Mum, I'm sorry,' I call out.

She doesn't look back.

Standing outside the gate I dial Neil's number with shaking hands, but the call goes straight to his answering machine. I leave a message. 'Neil, I need your help. You need to check on Mum. Things got out of hand. I just hit her. Could you please check on her? Please.'

I pass Edda. She is kneeling before a garden bed in her front yard, wearing bright green garden gloves.

'David,' she says. 'Are you all right?'

I don't answer, but get into my car and look in the mirror. The scratch is deep. I don't know if it was her ring or her nails that cut me, but it bleeds badly. I drive back to Newtown with an old towel pressed against my cheek.

I'm grateful to find a park right in front of the house. My legs are shaking as I walk across the backyard and once inside I collapse on a chair. A moment later I hear Pat at the door, but don't have the strength to get up.

She sits down next to me. 'Are you okay?'

I can't speak, just shake my head.

'That needs cleaning,' she says, looking at the scratch. 'It's deep.' She walks over to the kitchen and finds a first- aid kit in the cupboard.

Back at the table she pours iodine onto the gauze. 'It's going to sting,' she says. 'Do you want me to tell you something while I clean it?'

I nod.

She presses the gauze gently against my cheek and says, 'I always felt like I was too much growing up. Too loud, too extroverted.'

I try to resist the impulse to push her hand away.

'I went on my first school excursion when I was ten,' she continues. 'We drove to Katoomba. A bus full of inner-city kids who had never been out of the city.' She pours more iodine on the gauze and presses it onto the scratch again.

I wince.

'Are you okay?' She removes the gauze.

'Yes,' I say.

'When we finally stood at the lookout point in Katoomba, all huddled together in our green polyester uniforms,' she says, 'I felt like I was about to fly, and looking back I think it was my first experience of freedom. It was exhilarating. I started to giggle, but the headmistress looked at me as if I were mad. "There is nothing to laugh about, Pat," she said. "You'll get into trouble in life if you laugh at everything you see."' Pat puts the gauze down. 'Done,' she says. 'I think that's as clean as it will get.'

I lean over to kiss her the way I would Vera.

'You are so good at taking and appreciating,' Vera once said. 'Of letting yourself take without being a user.' And I take Pat's mouth now; unselfconsciously I taste her lips for comfort.

'No,' Pat says, pulling back. 'I don't want that.'

I sit back, feeling foolish. 'I'm sorry,' I say.

She looks at me, gauze still in her hand. Her eyes are clear as glass.

I want to add, 'It's habit. I didn't mean it,' but that will make no sense to her. I feel dizzy. The floorboards of the kitchen start to move and the smell of the iodine is over-powering. 'I'm sorry,' I say again.

I walk upstairs and hear Pat leave a moment after. Then my phone beeps on the table. There's a voice message from Vera.

'David,' she says. 'I'm standing in the garden, in our garden, and the light is so beautiful today.' Her voice sounds infinitely sad. 'I wanted to tell you that the fat possum that lives behind my studio fell off his branch this morning. He went right past the window and looked so surprised. It was such a funny moment and I wish…' She pauses, then says, 'this is our home, David. This is where you live. Please come home.' Then she hangs up.

I examine my cheek in the bathroom. The skin is swollen

and red, and standing next to the sink I swallow two Panadol. Then I stagger to the bed and lie down.

I long to get in the car and drive back home, but I can't. Vera will know straight away that I haven't given up on Ben. But as I drift off to sleep I allow myself to think about our house and the way it looks at dusk, light streaming through the windows.

The room is cold when I wake several hours later, and the blue curtain billows and sinks in front of the open window. But despite the cold I wake with the memory of a summer's morning when Ben was seven.

It was a hot morning and the window was open. It was still dark, but the first birds were already making a racket. And Vera had said something in her sleep.

'What?' I asked.

She mumbled into the sheet.

I turned to her. 'What's the matter?'

'Sorry?' she said sleepily.

'You were saying something.'

She stretched and moved closer to me. 'Did I wake you?'

'Yes.' I put an arm around her.

'I was dreaming.' She put her head on my arm. 'You were on a motorcycle without a helmet, racing down this road, shouting, "Too many kangaroos, too many kangaroos!"' She chuckled.

'Too many kangaroos?' I smiled with my eyes closed.

'Yes.'

'Did I look good on the bike?'

'Baby, you looked so handsome,' she said and moved closer.

She made a little sound getting on top of me. It wasn't a moan; it was a sound that carried something deeper. And the muscles of her thighs shifted as she moved. Maybe it was because I was only half-awake, but I felt a presence of love moving in us and outside of us. The experience was so strong that I wasn't able to answer when Vera asked if I was okay. All I could do was hold onto her. And then there was a knock on the bedroom door.

Vera pulled away from me, turned on the bedside light and drew the covers over us. 'Come in, darling,' she called out.

Ben was standing dressed in his school uniform, backpack in his hand.

'Why are you sounding funny?' he said.

Vera cleared her throat. 'We aren't sounding funny, sweetheart.' She sat up and looked at him. 'Ben, it's Saturday, there's no school today.'

'Yes, there is,' he said.

'No, not today, but you can play in my studio if you want and we can go for a bushwalk later.'

He started kicking the door, one little tap after another.

'I don't want to,' he said.

'Okay,' said Vera. 'Okay, you have to stop kicking the door. We'll find you something else to do.'

He kicked the door harder: bang, bang, bang.

Vera reached for her shirt and said to me, 'Why don't you make some coffee, and I'll get his toys. We can sit in the lounge under a blanket and drink coffee while he plays.'

I pulled on some shorts and walked past Ben without looking at him.

It's late afternoon and overcast when I wake. I have slept for hours and wince when I get out of bed. My cheek is sore and the painkillers have done nothing to ease my headache. That summer's morning with Vera seems so terribly long ago. I get the box of Panadol out and standing near the window I pop another two pills into my hand. And then I see Neil in the yard. He is sitting on the plastic table, head buried in his hands.

I open the window. 'Neil,' I call out.

He looks up. 'I knocked,' he says. 'I didn't think you were home.'

Neil is clearly drunk. He reeks of alcohol and as I fill the percolator and add coffee to the filter I wonder if it's even worth trying to get him sober.

'You knew she was leaving me,' he says and, in an

attempt to adjust himself, almost falls off the chair.

'Yes,' I say and put milk and sugar on the table.

'Why?'

'Why what?'

'Why did she tell you before me?'

'She wanted me to…to be there for you.'

The percolator starts to gurgle.

'Someone breaks into our house,' he says, 'breaks into our house, for fuck's sake, and she wants to leave. How does that make any sense? How does it go from A to fucking B like that?'

'She got scared,' I say and fetch the coffee.

'I know she fucking got scared, mate. She's my wife.'

I walk back to the kitchenette. 'Did you want something to eat?' I ask.

He rubs his forehead. 'I'm going to lose Jared.'

I grab a couple of green apples from the fridge and place them on the table, even though I am fairly sure Neil won't touch them. Whenever Maria lets him get away with it he subscribes to what he calls 'the low fruit and vegetable diet'.

'You're not going to lose Jared,' I say and sit down across from him. 'You will never lose him. He's your son.'

'I've put the biggest fucking lock on that door and now she wants to leave me. What am I going to do with that?'

'I don't know,' I say. 'Drink your coffee.'

'She got scared,' he says and drinks a big gulp of the coffee.

'Yes.'

Then his mouth quivers. 'It's more than that, isn't it?'

'I don't know,' I say, thinking that right now Neil looks about ten years old.

'I'm a failure, mate. I drink too much, and I'm not really good at what I do. I just pretend, I pretend all the time. Maria is the only fucking thing I got right.'

'Drink your coffee,' I repeat.

'David,' he says and his eyes start to flood.

I panic. 'Please, Neil. Please don't.'

But he begins to cry. He cries the way he did as a child: in great big sobs. It sounds like something pulled over a gravelly road.

Later I struggle getting him up the stairs. He falls into a fitful sleep on my bed and I stay next to him in a strange kind of vigil. He mumbles in his sleep, words unintelligible but full of pain. I sit in the stench of alcohol and remember the countless times he sat guard over me as a child and how I would go to sleep on his bed, listening to out-of-tune renditions of 'Hey Jude' and 'Sgt Pepper's Lonely Hearts Club Band'. I thought that he was the bravest brother anyone could ever have.

Now I sit for him, the purpose of which is not quite

clear to me. But I know that if I don't everything will come apart. I think of Neil crying and I think of my mother and the way she stumbled when I hit her. I think of Jared holding his teddy and of Pat pulling away from me in the kitchen. And I think of Vera alone in our house.

At dawn I walk downstairs and put on another jug of coffee. Neil joins me not long after with red eyes and stubbled cheeks. He pulls on his jumper while surveying the courtyard from the open doorway. 'Man, it's cold,' he says. 'Cold enough to freeze your nuts off.'

I let him joke, and we drink our coffee talking about King Street, the government, Shaggy's superior style on a surfboard. We talk as if we don't have a worry in the world, the way we did in our early twenties when we were intoxicated with youth, ideals and city life. But when Neil leaves he looks at me and I can see that it's all there, everything we didn't talk about, present and raw.

'Do you want to stay?' I ask.

He shakes his head. 'I need to be home. As long as she's there I need to be there too.'

I take a shower. Then I bring the bed linen downstairs and put it in the washing machine. Despite my lack of sleep I feel wide awake. I leave the house as the washing machine moves through its cycle with a low growl.

Pat's house is painted bright blue. As soon as I knock on the door I hear running footsteps and a dog barking. Eloise pushes the door open and an old poodle bounces out and begins to lick my hand.

'Muuum,' shouts Eloise. 'The man is here.'

Pat appears at the end of the hallway. 'I told you not to open the door,' she says to Eloise. 'Scotty, get back inside.'

'But Mum,' says Eloise, pulling her skirt further up her round belly, 'it's the man.'

'But you didn't know that before you opened the door, did you?' says Pat and sends me an apologetic look that makes me feel lousy.

'Okaaay,' says Eloise, then she is gone in a flash, down the hallway with Scotty.

'She is very sweet,' I say.

'Is everything all right?'

'Yes.'

'And your cheek?'

'It's okay,' I touch it instinctively. 'Still sore.'

'It was a bad scratch.'

'Look,' I say. 'I came because...'

'There's no need.'

'Please,' I say, 'let me apologise.'

'All right.' She stands aside. 'Come in.'

Pat covers a bowl of dough with cling-wrap and puts it in the fridge. She doesn't ask me to sit, but faces me across the kitchen table.

'I'm so sorry about what happened,' I begin. 'I didn't mean to kiss you, it wasn't something I was thinking about and then...did. It hadn't even occurred to me before it happened. Not that you aren't attractive, any man would notice you, it's just...'

'Please, stop,' says Pat.

'I'm not doing a very good job apologising,' I say.

'It's just a bit embarrassing.'

Eloise bounces into the kitchen with Scotty on her heels. She pulls at Pat's cardigan. 'Mum,' she says.

'Yes, darling?'

'We need to go to the park.'

Pat looks over at me. 'Do you want to come?'

We cram into her car, a beaten-up red Volkswagen, and drive to Camperdown Park.

'You don't walk?' I ask, when we get out five minutes later.

She shakes her head. 'Not with Eloise. She insists on saying hello to everyone we meet, dogs and people alike. And if she sees someone without teeth or someone who is carrying a little extra weight she's quick to point it out. Let's just say it's safer for all of us if we drive.'

I watch Eloise sprinting down the green lawn with the poodle. It's like seeing Ben as a child. He would run faster than his legs could carry him. Vera used to say that the only thing that kept him from falling was the desire to run, not the ability.

I haven't given up on you, Ben, I think. *Everyone else has, but I haven't.*

Eloise throws a green tennis ball with all her might. Scotty bounces after it and returns an instant later.

Pat puts a blanket on the ground near a row of swaying white gums.

'You said the other day that I was aloof,' I say and sit down next to her.

Eloise runs over to the graffiti wall. She climbs on a bench and throws the ball again.

Pat yells, 'Stay away from the bins.' Then she turns to me. 'Eloise saw a man looking through the garbage the other day, so now the bins have become irresistible.'

Someone starts mowing the lawn at the other end of the park. Above us the white gums catch the winter sun.

'I'm sorry I said you were aloof,' she says.

'What did you mean by it?'

'Do you really want to know?'

'Yes.'

'You just look like you have this secret life and that no one is allowed in.'

'You're pretty blunt.'

'I've already told you that.'

'I like it.'

'You're the first to say it.'

'I've always only opened up to one person,' I admit.

'Your wife?'

'Yes.'

'It must be lonely.'

'No,' I say. 'It never was. Not until now.'

She nods.

Eloise returns with the ball. It's covered in dog saliva.

'Give it to me, darling,' says Pat. 'I'll throw it.'

'Don't, Mum,' say Eloise. 'The sad man needs to throw.'

Pat looks at me and shrugs. 'The sad man needs to throw,' she repeats.

I take the ball and stand up. Scotty bounces around me.

'Are you ready?' I say to Eloise.

She nods seriously and then I throw as hard as I can. The ball goes past the bench, past the white gums, and Scotty charges after it.

Eloise looks at Pat, her eyebrows raised in exaggerated admiration.

'Yes,' say Pat and laughs, 'the sad man can throw.'

I sit back down on the blanket and watch Eloise run after Scotty.

'Is it true?' asks Pat. 'Are you sad?'

'I hit my mother yesterday,' I say. The words sound strange in my mouth.

'You hit her?' Pat looks at me.

Eloise waves at us and Scotty looks like he's about to have a heart attack.

'I've never hit anyone before,' I say. 'I feel ashamed.'

'Is she all right?'

'I don't know. I think so.'

'You need to apologise.'

'She doesn't deserve it,' I say and watch Eloise and Scotty's slow climb up the hill.

'Then do it for your sake,' says Pat.

Eloise comes over and flops down on the blanket. 'I'm hungry.'

We say goodbye in the park. Pat invites me for lunch, but I've already decided that it's time to look for Kaiser, Ben's friend.

'Thank you,' I say to Pat, standing next to the Volkswagen.

'For what?'

'For the park,' I say, 'and for not judging me.'

Wanders Cafe is wedged between an abandoned antiques shop and a vintage clothing store that sells 1950s dresses, bowties and two-tone shoes.

I squeeze through a small group of people chatting at the door and find myself a table near the window.

The waitress carries a notepad. Her sleeveless dress shows off her tattooed arms.

'Hey,' she says and glances at my cheek, 'what happened to you?'

'Better you don't know,' I say.

She reaches for the biro tucked behind her ear.

'May I have a flat white, please?' I ask. 'And some banana bread.'

'Sure thing, with butter?'

'Yes, please.' And then, like a bad detective, I ask, 'Is Kaiser working today?

'No,' she says. 'Did you want anything else?'

'Kaiser is a friend of my son's,' I say.

She glances at me over the notepad.

'Ben,' I add.

She puts the biro back behind her ear and studies me. 'You look alike,' she says. 'How is Ben? I haven't seen him since the day he walked out after that big row with the boss.' She glances over her shoulder and whispers, 'She had it coming by the way.'

'Ben's fine,' I say. 'I'm actually organising a surprise for him.' I feel bad about lying, but can't seem to stop myself. 'And I need to contact Kaiser. Do you know how I can get hold of him?'

'He doesn't work here any more. The idiot stole from the tip jar, how low is that?'

I wait.

'But he probably still lives around the corner.'

'Where?' I ask.

'Darley Street,' she says. 'Two streets down on the right-hand side. A three-storey terrace, yellow. You can't miss it.'

I knock on the door. Classical string music floats through the open window and blends with the smell of pot. Three bikes are chained together on the front verandah.

I knock again, harder this time.

A man in his mid-twenties opens the door. He has a blond goatee and his shirt hangs loose over his frame.

'I'm after Kaiser,' I say.

He glares at me. 'There's no one here by that name.'

There's something a little rehearsed about the way he says it.

'Do you know where I can find him?' I ask.

'Who are you?'

'I'm David, Ben's dad.'

His expression changes. 'Oh shit, sorry, man.' He shakes my hand. 'I'm Kaiser.'

'May I come in?'

'Of course, if you don't mind a bit of smoke.'

'I don't care,' I say.

I follow him down the hallway to a spacious kitchen. Dirty dishes are piled high in the sink, but the room is filled with exquisite Balinese teak furniture and a lavish fruit bowl is on display on the dining table.

'So why are you here?' He sits down and I follow suit.

A woman enters the kitchen and grabs a box of crackers from the kitchen bench. She is tall, with short brown hair.

'Hey, Lisa, they're mine,' says Kaiser.

She gives him the finger and leaves the room.

'How many people live here?' I ask.

'It depends.' Kaiser leans back in his chair. 'We have nine bedrooms, but at the moment there are only five of us. The house belongs to Lisa's parents,' he says. 'They're expats in Bahrain.'

'I was wondering if you could you tell me anything about the time just before Ben disappeared?' I say.

Kaiser shrugs. 'He had stopped coming over. To be honest I thought Lisa and him had a fight. It wasn't until I met Alice on the street that I found out what had happened.'

'Lisa? Who was just here?' I ask.

'Yeah. They used to be tight.'

'And you didn't see him during that time?'

'No,' he said.

'But you were friends.'

'We just hung out from time to time, that's all.' Kaiser picks up a banana from the fruit bowl and starts to peel it.

Lisa returns and puts the kettle on.

Kaiser turns in his chair. 'Hey, Lisa, this is Ben's dad.'

Only then does she look at me.

'Hi,' I say.

Lisa doesn't reply. Instead she leaves the kitchen abruptly.

'Hang on.' Kaiser gets up.

I hear him open a door and say, 'Lisa? Come on, babe. He just wants to talk.'

A few minutes later she appears in the kitchen doorway.

'I don't know what to say to you,' she says.

I stand up. 'Could we just talk for a moment?'

I follow her up the hallway and into her room. Kaiser seems to have disappeared.

She gestures to the only chair in the room. 'Have a seat.'

There are printed pages everywhere, laid out on the desk, the floor and the ancient-looking bed. She pushes some aside. The bed sags in the middle when she sits down.

'You and Ben were together?' I ask, with a sense of déjà vu.

'If you're here to tell me that I shouldn't have slept with Ben while he and Alice were still together, then please don't,' she says. 'Ben did break up with her eventually.'

'I don't care about that,' I say and look around the room. 'Do you play?' I nod at the French horn resting on the windowsill.

'Sometimes.'

'What else do you do?'

'Work in a call centre and talk to rude people all day, when I'm not trying to finish my thesis.'

'And what do you want to be?'

She looks at me as if trying to decide if I have any right to ask. 'Anthropologist,' she says. 'I'm doing my masters. I met Ben at uni.'

'Not through Kaiser?'

'It was the other way around.' She gets up, walks over to the desk and picks up a joint. 'Do you want some?'

'No, thanks,' I say.

She lights it, inhales and says, 'We met at the Manning Bar. The band that night was so bad, you have no idea— The Smashing Biscuits.'

'The Smashing Biscuits?'

'The name of the band. Ben and I bonded in disgust.' She pauses. 'You look so much like him,' she says.

'When did you last see him?' I ask.

'On my birthday. Just before...you know. We had

dumplings. Kaiser works at Dumpling King and brought home this huge box of leftovers. Ben gave me that heart.' She points to a purple glass heart leaning against the window next to the French horn. 'We talked and ate, and then he left. It was the first time he didn't stay the night. I wasn't upset, I knew it was going to happen sooner or later.' She looks at me. 'Everything was so intense with Ben, you know? He would make you feel like the most important person in the world, but then everything would change. I saw it happen with his friends, one after the other. Suddenly it was as if he could see all of it, you know? All the imperfections, all the flaws in people. And he got... disappointed. It was hard for him.' Lisa takes another puff of the joint, then says, 'We went there, you know.'

'Went where?'

'To the Gap.' She reaches for an ashtray on the floor. 'We took my car.'

'You asked him to go with you?'

'No,' says Lisa. 'He wanted to go. We went in the middle of the night and it was pitch black. All we could see was cliffs, you know, and a few lights from ships way out. And Ben went right up to the edge. I was shit-scared he was going to fall off, but he just stood there staring out into the night. "Imagine," he said, "imagine how it will look on the other side. Baby, the light will be so bright." I asked him what the fuck he was talking about and told him to get away from the edge.'

'What else did he say?'

'That's it. After that he was his usual self. We ate Mars Bars on the way and he sang me this crazy Tom Waits rendition of "Like a Virgin", it cracked me up. That was a week before my birthday, a week before I saw him the last time.'

It's raining again by the time I leave Lisa's house. The footpath is a sea of umbrellas and King Street smells of petrol fumes and cinnamon buns. I look around to see if I can spot a bakery nearby, but I can't see any.

I pass baskets with green-fleshed coconuts and ripe papayas outside a Fijian shop, and step aside to let a mother with a stroller pass. And right at that moment I see him again. Ben. He's walking a little further ahead and this time I can't lose him. This time I see him clearly. And I start to run; I weave in and out of pedestrians while keeping my eyes fixed on him. A dog barks and someone shouts, 'Watch out, dickhead.'

And he is right there, right in front of me. I grab hold of his arm.

'Ben,' I say and I have him. For a second I have him back and everything I need to say is right there in my mouth, in my breath, in the air.

He is younger than Ben. Same height, same hair colour,

but his face is narrow and his eyes a different shade of blue.

'Hey,' he says, 'get your hands off me.'

But I can't seem to let go of his arm.

'What the fuck is wrong with you? Get your hands off me.'

'Please,' I say. 'Please.' The disappointment is too much. I feel like I'm about to break in two.

He pulls his arm away from me. 'Fucking nutter.'

'I didn't mean...' I say, 'I thought you were my son.'

He straightens his sleeve. 'Why?'

'The way you walk. You look just like him.'

He shifts his backpack, then looks ahead and gives someone a wave.

I follow his gaze and see a young girl at a cafe table, straight brown hair and lipstick smile.

'Could you just stay for a moment?' I say.

He looks at me as if I'm crazy and I come to my senses.

'Sorry,' I say and step aside.

I look back to watch him bend down and swoop the girl up in an embrace, whispering something in her ear.

I walk down the first side street I come across and welcome the rain on my face. I walk blindly, passing apartment blocks and old factory buildings. Pools of water collect in the gutters and cars pass by, window wipers working frantically. And all I can think of is that morning in Moscow and how Vera was almost run over. She had dodged a snowball by running across the road, and had narrowly escaped being hit by a Škoda. I caught her on the other side with our three friends in sharp pursuit. 'Vera,' I said. 'Are you crazy? You could have been killed.' And she had put her gloved hands on my cheeks. 'I love you,' she said. 'And I'm alive.'

I no longer know where I am, but keep walking. And I think of the day when Ben was born and jackhammers shook the hospital wing, and then I think of his last morning alone. And I can't bear it. I can't bear to think that he would have travelled an hour on the bus knowing what he was about to do and not have called me. I can't bear that he might have felt completely and utterly alone.

I stop at a street corner and throw up on the shiny bitumen. Wave after wave of nausea rushes through me and I have no idea how long I'm standing bent over on the footpath. When the nausea finally eases I stand up and gingerly find my way back to the house. Everything feels as if it's come loose.

When I get back I ring Vera. I get her answering machine and say, 'It was never Ben.' Then I choke and can't say any more. I spend the rest of the day in bed unable to get warm. When darkness comes I finally fall asleep.

It's been raining throughout the night and King Street is

shimmering with moisture. A stray dog scuttles down the empty footpath, sidestepping puddles.

The whole block is quiet as I let myself into Ben's flat. I find a garbage bag in the kitchen and begin to pack. I pack his photos, the pink shirt, the guitar, his favourite mug and the old picture book. I try to do it as quickly as I can, but the pressure in my chest is getting worse. I put the bag down, and only just make it to the bathroom before I throw up again. Afterwards I sit on the toilet seat, thinking that perhaps I am having a heart attack.

Ben's blue towel hangs next to the sink. A bar of soap rests in the soap holder. And instead of ringing for help I undress clumsily and step into the shower. The hot water eases the pressure a bit. The soap smells of sandalwood and I wonder if it reminded Ben of India.

By the time I leave the flat King Street has come alive and there are people everywhere. Stalls are being erected for the weekend market and a busker sings huskily outside the closed bank, but I don't pause for any of it. I want to get back in the workshop with Ben's things and I want to finish the chest.

I trace the drawing on the front of Ben's childhood book. I do it slowly and carefully. A car passes on the lane outside. A ray of sun falls on the concrete floor. I place carbon paper on the timber lid and with the tracing paper on top

I print the image onto the wood. A small boy standing on the wing of a crop duster.

The indentation for the inlay needs to be nine millimetres deep, nothing more and nothing less. It's difficult to carve it by hand, but I prefer to do it this way. The process gives me time to imagine the inlay, and by the time I finish I know exactly what timber to use. I find a small piece of Brazilian rosewood, a piece of aged oak and a nice piece of creamy Japanese water chestnut.

Cutting the inlays into shape is precision work and takes time, but slowly the image comes together. When I place the last piece four hours have passed.

I walk up to King Street and have lasagne while I wait for the glue to dry. When I return to the workshop I sand the inlay, getting rid of marks from the carbon paper and any traces of glue. And then I rub it with methylated spirits and it comes to life. The lid still needs hinges and the whole chest needs to be oiled, but the inlay is magnificent.

At midday I drive to Leichhardt. There are Saturday shoppers everywhere and the cafes and bookshops are bustling. I can smell coffee, sharp and fragrant, as I get out of the car and walk down a side street to my mother's house. Her curtains are closed and there is no answer when I ring the doorbell.

I sit down and wait on the step. I close my eyes and let

the light catch my face. And I hear Ben's voice in my mind: *Once upon a time there was a little boy. All he wanted to do was to fly. Once upon a time.* Then I hear footsteps and look up.

My mother stands in front of me, striking as always in jeans and a bright blue coat. I can smell rosemary from her shopping bag.

I get to my feet and we stand in silence.

Then she asks, 'Do you want to come in?'

I shake my head.

'What are you doing here if you don't want to come in?'

A young boy flies past on his bike and at the same time, almost as if it was orchestrated, sprinklers turn on next door.

I reach out, slowly so as not to scare her, and put my hand on the cheek I hit. Her skin is soft and cold. She doesn't look at me, but presses her lips together. She keeps still even though I can feel she wants to move away. And something happens, something settles, in me, in her, and my hand stays on her cheek like a benediction. I close my eyes and for a moment everything is quiet.

'Are we going to stand here all day?' She draws back, but I see that something has changed. Her eyes have softened.

'Neil will need you,' I say. 'He's going to need all of us.'

'Neil?'

'Yes,' I say and then I leave.

Vera is waiting in the backyard when I return. She stands up as I walk through the squeaky gate.

'Vera,' I say.

She is wearing the old leather jacket again and I can't read the expression in her eyes.

'Would you like to come in?' I ask.

She nods.

I unlock the door. 'How long have you been waiting?'

'An hour.'

'Sorry.'

'You didn't know,' she says and follows me inside. 'What happened to your cheek?'

'Nothing,' I say and add, 'I'll tell you later.'

She looks as if she wants to say something, but is trying to figure out how.

'Would you like something to drink?' I ask.

'Maybe a glass of water.'

She walks into the workshop while I fill a glass at the sink.

I place the water next to her on the workbench and know that I won't be able to handle it if she has come to tell me that she is leaving.

'You packed his things?' She touches the frayed spine

of *Once I Had a Plane*.

'Yes.'

'The inlay is beautiful.'

'Thank you.'

'Let's go upstairs,' she says.

I follow her upstairs. The jasmine smells sweet and the drawn curtains colour the room blue.

'Something has changed,' she says. 'In you.'

'Yes.'

'What happened?' She reaches over and touches my cheek.

I almost start crying.

'Lie down with me,' she says.

Vera lies next to me on the bed. She is still wearing her jacket and I push away the memory of the other night when she slept fully clothed next to me.

'David,' she says.

'Yes.'

She doesn't speak, just looks at me and waits.

'Forgive me,' I say.

'For what?'

I am about to say, 'For not knowing what to do next,' but that's not what I am asking forgiveness for.

'For wanting him to be alive,' I say.

Her eyes fill.

'I wanted it so badly.'

She nods.

Something breaks in me and I can't breathe again. I try to cough, but it makes it worse. I want to tell Vera to call for help, that I need a doctor, but I can't get the words out.

'Vera.' I call out her name as if she is a thousand miles away, as if she is still standing at Red Square in Moscow on a winter's morning.

She puts a hand on my chest. 'It's okay.'

'I can't breathe.'

'You can,' she says, 'you are breathing, David. You are breathing, and you are here. You are here with me. Look at me.'

And I start to cry like a small child, with open mouth and clenched fists. And I hear Vera say, 'It's okay, it's okay.'

When I finally stop I squeeze her hand and get out of bed. Standing in the bathroom I splash cold water on my face and think of Ben. I think of him jumping off the cliff on that hot summer day and I hope he saw the horizon as he jumped. I hope he saw that line between sky and sea. I hope he saw the beauty that Vera talked about, because nothing else makes sense. It doesn't make sense that he is no longer, it makes no sense at all.

I return to the bed and lie down next to Vera.

'Hi,' she says.

'Hi.'

She sits up, takes off her jacket and jumper and her worn T-shirt that reads, 'Charlie Brown is my hero.' She's not wearing a bra and her jeans are loose around her belly. She has lost weight. The bed squeaks as she lies down again.

'Your turn,' she says.

I take off my sweatshirt, then lie back down. We look at each other. I dare not reach for her in case it breaks what's happening between us.

She pulls off her boots and pants, but keeps her briefs on. And then she waits.

I take off the rest of my clothes with shaking hands.

She looks at my erection and everything takes its own rhythm.

'I've missed you,' she says and moves closer.

'Your turn,' I whisper.

She pushes off her briefs. Her pubic hair is dark, her legs beautiful and shapely. I look at her, take her in as I reach over and ease my hand between her legs and then I kiss her. For a long time I kiss her.

'Now,' she says and I find her again. Her mouth, the

smell of her, my movements and the blue room, it all fits.

Afterwards I drift in and out of sleep. When I wake she is sitting at the edge of the bed pulling on her T-shirt. Fear rushes through me. Has she regretted what just happened between us? Is she about to tell me she's leaving? But when she turns I can see she's still with me.

'Come home,' she says.

I put a hand under her T-shirt and rest it on her warm hip.

She leans over and kisses me. 'Do we need to clean this place before we go?' she asks.

'I'll come back and do it later.'

Vera stands and stretches.

'Do you want a shower before we go?' I ask.

'Let's go home and wash in the creek instead,' she says.

We leave the city with the chest and Ben's things on the back seat. We drive through the hills of Richmond, past the apple plantations of Bilpin and past the fields with the Appalachian horses. Every bit of road is familiar and takes us closer to home. Our lovemaking sits between us and before us clouds lift and shift in the horizon. We drive past the place where we bought the strawberries. The memory shimmers like a ghostly fata morgana at the side of the road. I glance at Vera. And I know she sees it too.

The bush is quiet as we walk down to the creek. Twigs break, leaves rustle, but otherwise everything is still. I breathe in the fragrant smell of the bush as we descend deeper and deeper.

Vera takes my hand when we reach the bottom and we cross the creek, one stone step at a time.

We take off our clothes standing on the flat rock near the waterhole and Vera gets in first. 'Oh,' she says. 'It takes your breath away.' Then she walks further out until she stands waist deep.

You take my breath away, I think as I walk out to stand next to her in the freezing water.

'It's too cold,' she says. 'I feel like I'm having a heart attack.'

Two cockatoos call out as they pass above us. They're moving north.

I reach over and take her hand. I raise it high in the air as if we are the winners of some bizarre sporting competition.

'What?' She smiles just a little.

'I don't know.' I smile back, our arms sink. 'We're here. It's a good day.'

'Let's do it,' she says. 'On three.'

ACKNOWLEDGMENTS

Writing a novel is like weaving a giant tapestry: a tapestry of stories, a sense of purpose and a huge amount of inspiration. It's also a long process and without good friends and expert support this novel may never have seen the light of day.

So thank you to my wise and wonderful friends for their feedback and their support: Vicki Hansen, Associate Professor Anne Brewster, Angela O'Keeffe, Dr Prue Gibson, Thomas Larsen, Narelle Jones, Elizabeth Gorringe and Dr Meredith Jones. And a very special thanks to Simone Fraser for the time she spent reading various drafts, as well as for her insight and kindness.

My gratitude to Dr Barry Webb for his superior listening skills. You let me talk until I found the missing thread, and you probably didn't even know how helpful this was.

Many thanks to Matilde Martin and Josef Ber for the many inspiring conversations, but most of all for being family.

I am grateful to Associate Professor Hans Skov-Petersen. Thank you for the lift and for the great conversations we had in the car. You impressed upon me the fact that no one is born with a sense of direction, regardless of what we might like to think. This sparked off several ideas that would later make it into this book.

My deep gratitude to Michael Heyward at Text.

Thank you for your ever-present guidance, but especially for your faith in the dreaming that comes before a book. Every writer should have a Michael in their life.

Many thanks also to Alaina Gougoulis at Text. You made the editing process such a joy and the book the very best it could be.

I am indebted to Stephen Gibson and Alison Chamberlain. Thank you for the time spent in your exquisite furniture shop, Original Finish in Newtown, and for generously giving me material to draw from in regards to woodwork and furniture design.

Many thanks to Richard Crosland at School of Fine Woodwork in Alexandria for his hospitality. I loved the smell of sawdust as you enlightened me about the process of an inlay. You were most patient and kind.

And last, but not least, I am tremendously thankful to Clinical Professor Jo Duflou at Sydney University for his time and thorough answers to all my questions relating to forensic pathology and coroner practices, and to Sergeant Kylie Whiting, team leader of the Missing Persons Unit, NSW Police Force, for providing me with all the information needed to make this story as real as possible. Thank you very much to the both of you, for your help as well as for your service.